Praise for Refugee Tales

'*Refugee Tales* is a wonderful way of re-humanising some of the most vulnerable and demonised people on the planet. This collection is both challenging and poignant. Readers will surely be moved to move their leaders to action.'
– Shami Chakrabarti

'We hear so many of the wrong words about refugees – ugly, limiting, unimaginative words – that it feels like a gift to find here so many of the right words which allow us to better understand the lives around us, and our own lives too.'
– Kamila Shamsie, author of *Home Fire*

'In sparse language we hear with a heart-wrenching immediacy and intimacy of brutalities and injustices of refugee life in Britain, but also of hope and optimism in the hardest circumstances.'
– Kerry Hudson, *The Big Issue*

'A courageous book, it offers the reader great solace. It gives faces to the faceless, and voices to the voiceless, humanizing the people that our society demonizes.'
– Jackie Kay, author of *The Lamplighter*

'The best arguments I have ever read – albeit through tears – for why asylum is not a privilege but a right.'
– Gillian Slovo, author of *An Honourable Man*

'This stark short story collection will shake you to the core.'
– *Reader's Digest*

'The sensitive and extremely poignant way the accounts are communicated does them the justice they deserve.'
– *The Morning Star*

'All the tales in the two volumes are at once deeply personal and "world-sized", and the question of how best to convey both their specificity and their representativeness is clearly a significant one for the writers involved.'
– *The Glasgow Review of Books*

'As a witnessing of a hidden humanitarian crisis within the UK, the stories are necessary and compelling; purely on the merit of the writing, they are an excellent read. The telling of the stories is varied, but all are told with respect and a sense of responsibility to their subjects.'
– *Wasafari*

'Humanises a crisis often rendered in statistics.'
– *The Economist*

REFUGEE TALES

VOLUME IV

Edited by
David Herd & Anna Pincus

A CIP catalogue record of this book is available from the British Library.

ISBN 1912697483
ISBN-13 978-1-91269-748-9

Proceeds from this book go to the following two charities:
Gatwick Detainees Welfare Group and Kent Refugee Help.

The publisher gratefully acknowledges the support of Arts Council England.

Supported using public funding by

**ARTS COUNCIL
ENGLAND**

Printed and bound in England by Clays Ltd, Elcograf S.p.A

MIX
Paper from
responsible sources
FSC® C018072
www.fsc.org

Contents

CONTENTS

Prologue

The Time Traveller's Tale

as told by

Shami Chakrabarti

So MUCH IS MADE of individual 'genius'. Yet I have benefited a great deal from cooperation and dialogue in my life and career. I am proud to acknowledge how friends like Marcel Grossmann, Michele Besso and Nathan Rosen aided my understanding of the physical universe. My conversations and correspondence with Charlie Chaplin, W. E. B. Du Bois and Sigmund Freud amongst numerous others, helped my understanding of our man-made and inner worlds. Yet it is my still necessarily anonymous collaborator to whom I perhaps owe the most. For whilst I have been credited with outlining a path for time travel with my famous theories, it is she who made the most practical advances in this area and put them flamboyantly to the test, even to the point of coming back to discuss them with her forbear in discovery. It is not my place to discuss her method. I have sworn not to do so for fear of a regret as great as the one I feel about signing that letter to Roosevelt urging atomic weapon research in 1939. What I am discussing here, is something of what I have learned of the past and future, as places and possibilities in themselves.

If, as I believe, war is a disease, then the one from which the world emerged ten years ago was like a deadly global pandemic. It will be widely remembered for the longest time and well into the next century. Yet, as is perhaps the way with human memory, the battles, bombs, heroism and uniforms will sometimes be venerated more than the underlying values for which that war was fought and won by those opposed to fascism, race-discrimination and inhumanity. As a result, it will be some time before one of the greatest treasures of the subsequent peace is properly valued and protected. I speak of the Refugee Convention of 1951. This document is very dear to me as I have always preferred an international legal order to perpetual war. Also, I was a European refugee in 1933, refused asylum in the United Kingdom before accepting refuge here in the United States of America.

Did you know that advanced Western European countries used to incarcerate the poor in so-called debtors' prisons? Imagine the cruelty and futility of that. And yet, well into the next century, many nations will imprison those seeking asylum with either no due process rights at all, or with far inferior fair trial protections to those afforded people accused of serious crimes. As I have said before, the very definition of insanity is 'doing the same thing over and over again and expecting different results.'

That incarceration will often be indefinite in nature and some people, including families with children, will be imprisoned for years on end, in a variety of formal prisons, euphemistic 'detention centres' and 'facilities', in refugee camps and even cages. Yes, that will happen even in the enlightened world of the 21st century and even after men have walked on the moon, women taken full ownership of their own bodies and people can both communicate and unlock nearly all of recorded human history and learning via keyboards and screens. But 'two things are infinite: the universe and human stupidity; and I am not sure about the universe.'

This policy will obviously come at a very heavy price for these prisoners of the future, but it will cost the nations they have fled, those to which they have escaped and wider humanity as well. For these people are scientists, teachers, thinkers, activists and public servants, just as I was, when I was offered a position in American and world society instead of a prison cell in my new home or certain death in my original one.

But out of adversity comes opportunity, and whilst the first quarter of the next century will bring great turmoil, it will also bring great catalysts of change. Movements to save our precious planet, its people and its soul will come together to form an irresistible force for greater peace, equality and sustainability within one generation. People of science, culture and civic action will come together and along the way, some of the barbarism will be consigned to the primitive curiosities of that place called the past, alongside debtor's prison and beliefs in racial supremacy.

I leave this message in the hope that it is found by some good people of imagination to whom the knowledge may provide some encouragement. But I hope you will remember that, 'imagination is more important than knowledge. Knowledge is limited. Imagination encircles the world.'

A. Einstein, Princeton 1955 (well, perhaps...)

The Hotelier's Tale

as told to

Robert Macfarlane

HOW BEST CAN I help you tell your story?
    I don't know which part of my story is very interesting for you?
    All of it.

★

I was born with mountains around me.

I was born on the first day of a month, in the first year of a decade, more than two kilometres above sea level.

The mountains of my childhood are green, even at their tops – and they are high. Cold and rain sweep them in winter, but there is almost never snow. No wonder so many famous runners come from this part of my country! It is a beautiful landscape. I love where I grew up, of course. Who cannot? It is where our first memories are made, and mine were made among mountains.

Mountains keep a different time, a deeper time. Their time is more like God's, and it does not run in straight lines.

★

The clock is clicking. I can hear every movement of the thin red second hand. *Click. Click. Click.*

Time is two kinds of enemy when you are in this system. As the first enemy, time slows, thickens, becomes sticky. It is something you wade in. As the second enemy, time rushes onwards, forwards. It is a flash flood in the mountains, forcing you helplessly towards a precipice.

I go to the Home Office in London as I do every month, to sign the form which proves I am still here, which tells them that they do not need to come looking for me. But this month it is not like other months. Suddenly they tell me to go through a door, to the next room, behind the main office.

I am not ready for this.

There are men there, waiting for me. There is a clock on the wall with a thin red second hand.

I am not ready for this.

They keep me in the office for three hours, then they take me in a van to the detention centre. I have my bag, the clothes I came in, my phone, my watch. Nothing else. I am given no reason for my move to this centre, but I know what it means. It means they want to fly me back to my country. The plane will come in over the mountains which will be green even at their tops, and it will land at the airport, and the authorities of my country will be waiting to take possession of me

I am not ready for this.

*

I grew up with mountains around me.

My parents were civil servants. I went to school in our city in the mountains, and when I had finished school I trained to be a teacher. For ten years I worked in a primary school in a village out in the countryside, some distance from our city, perhaps five or six hours' walk from the nearest bus stop.

I taught everything! Maths, languages, geography, history… It was happy chaos. I remember the sound of chalk on blackboard. I remember the sight of the dust in the air where the sun shone into the classroom. There were 40 or 50 students in my class, sometimes even more, of different ages. Two hundred or three hundred students in the school as a whole, aged from six to eleven. They would come from the villages around my village. Some of the very small children would walk an hour each morning to school, and an hour back home each evening. Some of the older children even ran to school, barefoot. It made them all so strong.

Life seemed endless then. Time flowed steady; a slow river with broad banks, no eddies. I was young and cheerful in those years. I enjoyed giving knowledge to those who wanted it. It was my first experience outside my family, in the countryside. After school, we teachers would play football or volleyball together, or just sit and talk. The children would walk back to their families each afternoon, and return each morning. They were our clock, our time-keepers.

★

The clock is still clicking. *Click. Click. Click.*

In the detention centre, I am given my first 'ticket'. *Tick, tick, ticket.*

My ticket tells me the precise day and time of my deportation flight. My solicitor appeals. She submits the right documents. To my joy, the ticket is beaten. The ticket is cancelled! But still they do not let me leave the centre.

So I wait. After a week, they give me another ticket. Oh, this is a hard day. My solicitor tries again, but she cannot cancel the second ticket. One day before my deportation date, my solicitor tells me that she has given up on my case. *I have tried everything I can*, she says, *but nothing has worked. There is nothing more I can do, so I must leave you.*

I am not ready for this.

She has one last suggestion, but I can tell from the way she says it that it is meant to make her feel better rather than to make me feel hopeful. She says, *You can go to the Royal Court of Justice and apply personally for a review of your case.*

To the Royal Court of Justice? In person? From here? With one day to go before my flight?

Time is a torrent and I am caught in its current.

★

After ten years of teaching in the village, I decided to change my profession and my life. I could not have known then how very changed it would become. I left the village and my hometown, and I came to the university in the capital of my country to study marketing. I studied for four years, and then I joined a company in the capital. Three years went by. I decided to start my own business, so first I ran a shop, and then I moved again, this time to a city in the south of my country.

There I rented a hotel and I began my business as a hotelier, welcoming tourists, business people, international visitors. To the west of my hotel was a great river. To the south was a great low-lying desert. And at the front of my hotel was a great valley. When I looked out of the windows of my hotel, I looked millions of years back in time.

There, above the valley, I began to read books about politics. I borrowed them from friends, and I began to discuss politics with others in the city. A small group of us would share magazines and books, sending them to one another. We decided to become supporters of the opposition political party, which was in exile. In the group, we were five people. Politics drew us together.

You ask why I did this? Because when you read, you come to know what is right and what is wrong, and you must follow this knowledge. Of course, we understood that our meetings were dangerous. We were aware of what they do to those who support the opposition party. But sometimes you do these things because you must.

One day, the five of us were at a meeting in a residential area. It all happened very fast, in a rush. The door was kicked in. *Bang.* The security forces raided the room and arrested all of us.

★

I cannot go to the Royal Court of Justice because I am being held in the detention centre. You cannot just… walk out of the centre! It has razor-wire on its fences. It is a place designed to keep people in once they are there. The next morning, the day I am to be deported, they come to my room and tell me that I will be taken to the airport at 3pm.

I am not ready for this.

There is only one chance left. My friend agrees to go for me to the Royal Court of Justice. To write a letter, fill out the forms, and travel to the Royal Court of Justice to submit them. An interpreter will help him. We know it will not work, but what else can you do? Maybe the court will have time to see it and give a response to the Home Office to stop my deportation. Maybe. We have only a few hours. *Click, click, click.*

When I was a young man I visited the churches in the north of my country. Eleven churches were cut out of the rock there. The churches live among the mountains. The churches are perhaps 600 years old. The rock into which they are cut is maybe 20 million years old.

As I have told you, I am very trustful with my God. Whatever happens, happens. That's my belief. On some days – like the day of my deportation – I am not happy, but I know I have to trust with my God.

★

After the security forces arrested us, we were taken to a big political prison that was well known for the terrible things that happened within it. It is closed now, I am happy to say. I was held without trial there for a year. I was treated badly, of course, because I was a political prisoner. Yes, they tortured me. They interrogated me, they tortured me, they did anything they wanted to me, in order to know about the secrets of the opposition party. I was with my four friends at first in that prison, but after we were split up, well, I have not heard of them again.

Time, in that place? It pooled sticky on the floor.

While I was in prison, my wife could not run our hotel alone and look after our two children, so the business closed. She returned to the capital. My children are now ten and seven. I have not seen them for the last two and a half years. Nothing hurts more than this. No time is slower than the time I spend away from my children.

I was held without trial, of course, but after a year they released me on bail, and with a ban preventing me from taking part in any political action or conversation. After some months, in secret I re-joined the opposition party. I began again to help the exiled opposition party communicate within the country.

You wonder why I became involved in politics again, despite the risk? It is simple. Because, in my understanding, it was completely wrong and undemocratic what the government was doing. I wish that my country would be a free country. If I believe this, I have to contribute something. I wish freedom for my country – but wishing is not enough.

Soon I was told that the security forces knew I had become re-involved with politics. I did not wait for them to find me. I went into hiding.

★

The hour is going on. The hour is counting. *Click, click, click.* I wait in the detention centre for a call from my friend. There is no time to achieve something, so what can I do but wait? Nothing. Nothing to do but wait.

Each second is heavy as a single stone. Each second falls, and slowly the stones build up around me.

Nevertheless, I am calm as the stones rise, because I have done what I have done. Up to the maximum point, you will do your best – and then finally you give up and become calm.

Hope is not what you need beyond the maximum point, for there hope pulls you back.

My friend calls me and tells me to send some more documents. So I go to the library in the detention centre, where it is free to write e-mails, and I send scans of my documents for him to take to the Royal Court of Justice. I am sending the last document when the guard comes through to me and taps me on the shoulder, and tells me that the people are waiting for me now.

I am not ready for this. The stones have reached my throat now.

Don't worry, I am coming, I say, *but let me send only this paper.* So the guard waits for me in the library and I send it, and then he takes me away.

★

My wife was not safe from the government at the beginning when I went into hiding. She was interrogated by the police three or four times as to my whereabouts. She did not tell them, though she knew very well where I was. I was on their watch-list. *Tick, tick, tick.*

I hid in a village a hundred kilometres away from the capital. I stayed inside all of this time. No one could see me, except the relatives who kept me safe. Every day I was worried I would be discovered. Each day I felt I was walking on a bridge made of glass. But each day also joined to the next, and the next, to become a single day that stretched away without an end. I was away from my family, and I knew I had no safe future in my country, and I did not know which country I could live in.

It was like trying to cross a wide desert of soft, soft sand on foot.

★

The guard takes me straight to the office at the detention centre, and there are four people waiting for me: two guards, one doctor, one manager. They are all going to fly to the capital of my country with me. They are going to… *deliver* me.

They are very professional. The guards have handcuffs. If I resist they will handcuff me. They are friendly people. If I resist, they will change to become unfriendly. But I am not ready to fight, because it is meaningless to fight. The stones are over my head now. Whatever happens, I am prepared to accept it, because God has willed it.

For the first time in a long time, the ticking has stopped. The red second hand sweeps round smoothly now.

They search me from up to down, they search my bags from left to right, and then we all get into a van and we drive together to Heathrow. We leave the centre at 4pm, and my flight leaves at 7pm. But the traffic is very easy, so we get there too early.

They say we can have some coffee and some chicken. *Would I like some,* they ask? *Are you OK,* they ask? What can I say to this? I can't say anything. So we go back out of Heathrow, and in the van, they bring me coffee and chicken.

★

While I was hiding, my brother arranged everything so that I could leave.

When the moment was right, I came to the airport. There, my brother had bribed the right officers. It was cheaper this way. If I tried to travel to a neighbouring country by land, I would pass through ten checkpoints, or twelve. It is harder and more expensive to bribe so many people. One person at the airport? Two? Less risky, less complicated.

I flew to Paris. The brokers in Paris had arranged everything. There was a stranger there to welcome me. He had my photo, and he came to me, as I was expecting. I spent five days in Paris, while people arranged my next journey. Finally, they decided to send me to Holland. But wherever the plane landed first, there I must tell my story to immigration officers.

You ask why I did not stay in France? It is because the French government is experienced with sending people back to its good friends in the government of my country.

I flew to Southampton. I was meant to be going to Amsterdam. At Southampton I told the immigration officers who I was. They arrested me. They took my passport. They tried to send me back to France, I think, but they could not.

I was sent to a hostel in Croydon for a week, then I was sent to Cardiff for long-term accommodation. I was in Cardiff for more than a year. I was given £35 a week. In Cardiff I applied for asylum. They interviewed me, and I told them everything I had gone through, and finally they denied me. They did not accept half or more of what I told them, so they refused me asylum.

It all depends on who interviews you. I had one interviewer, who spoke to me for two hours. He had no specialist knowledge of my country. Perhaps he might have googled the name of my country after the interview, or even before. He was kind in the moment, but in the end he was without mercy.

What I wanted to tell him, what I wanted to make him see, was the simplest fact of all, the proof of the truth. Why would I leave my children behind if my life was not in danger, if my life did not put them in danger? That is the only truth that is needed for my story.

I am always thinking about my children. They are growing up. Every day they are one day older. This is the clock that I cannot stop. In the future, if they are seventeen or eighteen, they are no longer my children, and they will never have known me. My regrets rise when I am thinking about this, when I am thinking like this. My God cannot help me here. Time, as do my children, hurts me so much. This chance with them will not come again. This is once in a lifetime.

This is a problem.

★

When the time approaches for my deportation flight, we drive back to Heathrow. The coffee is all drunk and the chicken is all eaten. Now and then the manager is checking his phone, to see if it is still going ahead, to see if there is any message. He knows, because I have told him, that my friend is at the Royal Court of Justice. He tells me that he has a secure means of communicating with the Home Office, so that at any time if the decision arrives, we will know it.

There is one more stone that needs to be placed on me. Only one. My eye can still see from this last gap, where the last stone is missing.

I am very calm because I have tried everything. I have concluded that it is the will of God that I will fly in over the mountains which are green to the top, to be delivered to the men who will be waiting for me at the airport. So this is the nature of my trust. I was with my God for all of these hours and minutes.

We must check in at Heathrow. But the coffee means that I need the toilet. There is thirty minutes to check in. Even in the toilet I cannot be alone! One of the guards follows me into the toilet, and holds the door with his hand while looking away. The manager comes in also, to wait just outside.

And then the manager's phone rings.

Ring, ring, ring.

★

The year and a half after I was denied asylum were very hard. My solicitor took my case to judicial review, but in that time I had no accommodation, no money, no help, nothing. I could not have survived without the kindness of strangers.

I stayed in Cardiff for some months with friends, supported by NGOs who cared for refugees. I met such kindness from them. The Red Cross. The Catholic Missionaries. The Jesuit Refugee Service is a special place. They have a legal department, and they will go through all your documents and send them to the solicitors. I have now submitted my second judicial review thanks to them. Without these organisations, I could not have survived.

Finally, last January they gave me this accommodation in London, because my second judicial review is now underway. But I cannot withdraw money any longer. I can only pay for food. I have £35 a week on which to feed myself. And that is it. They are making things tougher for me. This is the hostile environment. But it is nothing like the hostile environment I will face in my country.

So I am staying. I am waiting.

★

The manager's phone is ringing! I say to myself – *this is my call! It is God on the phone! Trust in God!*

And when I come out of the toilet, all of these people cry *Congratulations!* The manager has heard from the Royal Court of Justice. My friend has been successful for me. The guards, they embrace me. *Only thirty minutes from check-in,* they say! *Can you believe it?* they ask.

I cannot believe it. I cannot thank them. I cannot hug them. I just stand. I just stand.

So they drive me back to the detention centre again. We arrive there and the people there are very happy to see me. They call my name. *Oh, you came back!* they say. *Good news!* they say. *We have kept your room,* they say, *we have not had time to give it to someone else!*

The next day I am told that I have a call from the Home Office. *They want to talk to you.* I am wondering what will happen next. A third ticket? I travel to see them face to face. They tell me that I do not need to return to the detention centre. I do not ask why. I just leave. They give me a train ticket to King's Cross. I get off there, and I walk freely through the streets of London.

★

Now I spend my days mostly reading the Bible, and reading books. I spend most of my time in the local library, but it is closed for two days a week, so on these days I go to the Red Cross. It has tea, coffee, food, and people gather there so I can spend time talking with other refugees and asylum seekers. The coffee is bad, but the conversation is good.

Meanwhile, I am waiting. My papers have gone in for a judicial review. This process will confirm whether my asylum case has been fairly looked at. If not, the Home Office will have to reconsider the application.

So my life is lived now mostly in the present.

I go to church, for there is an Orthodox Church in London. My faith is so important. It is very difficult to think of going through this without faith

I speak to my wife and my children. I speak to them on the phone. I see their faces across such great distance.

I think about my time, what I have learned. Most people from my country have a misunderstanding of the exile life in Europe or America. I was like them. I didn't expect such difficulties! I have faced such strong challenges in my life here. Never such challenges before, even in prison.

Our assumption is that you will come and be made welcome in these countries. That has not been the case. However, in other ways my welcome has been beyond expectation. Some people here are so kind and welcoming; they will share everything. Especially these charities. The people there give us accommodation for free, breakfast and dinner for free. They even wash our bedsheets with their hands, the sisters clean the toilets with their hands. They are so kind – and when you look at such people you will be filled with positive feelings. But the system... the system is unexpectedly very strong and very unwelcoming.

I dream that if the Home Office grant it, then I can bring my family and we can live together here in the UK.

I think of my story. My story is part of my life. I enjoyed it in some ways. Because my challenge has its own test. I am growing stronger and stronger.

Some people tell me, *You do not seem to be part of what is happening to you.* They see I am calm and peaceful and happy. *But you are in a very difficult situation, how is it that you seem so calm?* they ask. They are wrong. I tell them that I am in this situation, but I am not only living in it. I am living out of it. Sometimes the river rushes me on towards the edge. At other times I stand looking down at its flow.

I must not think about where I am all the day long. For it is not permanent. I do believe everything will pass. My teaching has passed, my business has passed, my detention has passed, and I hope tomorrow will be another wonderful day. I am always waiting, but I am always trying to use the days. Each day, rather than worry, I see that whatever comes, comes.

I am ready for this.

I have nothing to lose.

When the time comes, I will paint my house.

My family is the thing that makes time difficult for me.

I speak to them once a week, at the weekends.

My children are at school now.

They do not run because in the big cities there is no space to run.

They cannot see the mountains from where they are.

I am waiting.

I am always waiting.

The Teenager's Tale

as told to

Maurizio Veglio

A Beginning

I LIKE DRIVING. I always did, since I was a kid. At thirteen I stole the keys of my father's car in Riyadh. In Saudi Arabia, all boys drive by the age of fifteen. It was my first time; I couldn't even slow down before turning. I messed up but managed to drive for about ten minutes. Then I drove back home and tried to park in the same place from where I left. I hit a wall with the side of the car. My father yelled at me, furious, but a few days later he let me drive again, to learn.

It was not too difficult, in fact. There are wide streets in Riyadh, suitable for big and long cars. In Italy, however, streets are tiny, and so are the cars. It really takes a lot to become familiar and to avoid mistakes. And the process, I know for sure, can be painful.

A Centre

What am I doing in this centre? There are four-metre-high fences, a plain courtyard in each area, five identical low prefabs, each hosting seven people. Walls are scratched and covered with writings, some prefabs are burnt. Toilets are inside the rooms, but have no doors. We are all foreigners, here. They call us undocumented migrants. Sans-papiers. Clandestini. When I entered this place, the Turin pre-removal detention centre, a man from the staff speaking Arabic looked at me and said: 'If you are Somali, they can't deport you. But you will have to stay here for some months.'

The centre is packed with North Africans. I saw very few of them around Europe. They all seem to have gathered here, and Nigerians too. The main language inside the camp is Arabic. Now I can understand all of them and I can tell which country someone has come from. Arabic is the lingua franca.

Guards are all around us. If you need to see the doctor, if the lawyer is coming to see you, if they call you at the Migration Office, a number of policemen will come and escort you. You are never alone in the camp, but you live in isolation. And there is nothing to do inside here. Time is tough and heavy. Waiting raises the pressure. But I can handle it, I learned to be patient.

Sometimes a fire breaks out: police come running and push everyone as if we were all criminals, force us to a different area or into the canteen where we eat. Some people in detention had to sleep there on the floor. The food is terrible, by the way. And if the canteen is out of order, we eat in the prefab, on the very bed where we sleep. But at least you are not eating alone. I know things about this place. It is my third time here. I am twenty-six years old.

A House

What am I doing in this house? At fourteen I should be hanging around with friends, playing football and driving my father's car. Instead, I'm stuck in this apartment in Mogadishu, unsafe and uncomfortable. Even my family is worried for me. A few weeks ago, after the prayer at the Mosque, I was addressed by an old sheikh. He asked me a lot of questions about my roots, my family, my strange accent. And he questioned me on religion and politics: what did I think about those 'Ethiopian soldiers' attacking the great State of Somalia? What did I think about the fighters defending the nation from foreigners? He introduced me to some young men, 20-25 years old. He said they were all ready to sacrifice their life to defend Somalia, they were good examples. I did not know what to think.

Some days later, I met one of the young men in my neighbourhood. He told me the group was monitoring me and that I had to decide either to join them or to leave the country. He added that if they ever discovered that I was passing information to other people they would kill me.

The next encounter was the last one. Another boy from the same group – I guess they were all from Al Shabaab – publicly called me a spy, someone who came to Somalia to collect information and report them elsewhere. They attacked me, wounded me on my right knee and threatened me with death.

This is why I'm living like a prisoner in solitary confinement. My family does not want me to leave the house. By the way, I'm also new to the place. I was born and raised in Riyadh and lived there until a few months ago. My friends are all there. I liked it more than Mogadishu. Here everything looks dangerous: checkpoints, weapons, uniforms. I am waiting for my uncle's call to leave for Ukraine. I really hope it will not take too long.

A Private Car

What am I doing in this car? We are four in number, one of us is a girl. It is a long drive; we are fleeing across a country. We spent the last two days walking behind two men in military dress. We were trespassing, crossing the border between Ukraine and Slovakia. Smugglers arranged some cars to Bratislava and then Wien. I am fifteen years old.

In Wien we see a woman wearing a hijab. She speaks Arabic, she's Egyptian. 'Today is Friday, I'll take you to the mosque. There you will meet other Somali.' After taking the prayer we see our community. You always find good people: they know what we are going through and some of them make an arrangement for us. They take us to an empty house and let us stay: 'You pay if you can, if you can't, you will pay later.' We stay for two weeks in Wien, then I move to Germany. I'm heading to Norway, where my cousin lives. I have never met him but we talk on the phone; he knows I am coming.

The Somali community is like a GPS. Most of them have faced the same conditions, which is why they help each other. They understand the situation. I take a bus to Hamburg, change in Copenhagen and Malmö, then I reach Oslo, where my cousin is waiting for me. Living in his place, I meet a lot of Somali at shops, playgrounds, public places. We visit each other and eat together. I also have Egyptian and Sudanese friends, because I speak good Arabic. They help me in applying for asylum, but my request is denied. I am still fifteen years old.

A Prison

What am I doing alone in this cell? When I entered the prison, everyone was pointing their eyes and fingers towards me. They saw me on TV, apparently. I did not expect it; if you do nothing wrong you do not expect it. They knew nothing about me, and yet: 'He's the most dangerous,' 'He's the most dangerous.' Day and night, I could hear their whispering.

I was held in solitary confinement for two months, in a plain cell with no TV. Then I was moved to another cell, this time with a TV. That's how I learned Italian. I understand more than I speak, because I listen more than I talk. And here nobody speaks English. I'm not a sociable guy, so when they try to put me in a cell with someone else, I refused: I prefer to be on my own. I was still able to see and talk to other inmates in high security; there used to be another Somali next to my cell, with whom I joked a lot, and a man from Macedonia too. Now we are about 30 people in the section, but we never meet all together. And you never leave the section unless someone pays you a visit – very rarely, as far as I am concerned.

The daily routine is like a circle: breakfast alone in the cell; one hour in the sport area; one hour playing cards or table-tennis in the hall; lunch in the cell, alone again; two hours in the hall and dinner, then alone once again. It is now two years since I entered the high security prison, when I was twenty years old. Almost everyone here is a foreigner. Half of them are claiming innocence, some get acquitted and released after years of detention; most get deported at some point. From time to time I do little jobs, like food distribution or cleaning. And I get books, a good number of them.

Sometimes I look back at what happened before, when I was in the reception centre. They hid a camera in my room and later on they showed me videos. I did nothing wrong, I never had weapons nor attacked anyone, but they claimed I was inciting people to jihad. At the trial, most testimonies were in my favour but the prosecutor and the judge did not listen to them. They even turned some jokes we used to make amongst ourselves into actual threats. They had already sentenced me on TV, how could they change their mind?

A Police Car

What am I doing in a police car? A Pakistani guy and I have been spotted and stopped by Austrian policemen and they are taking us somewhere, again. I was walking with Google Maps on my phone, the phone in my hand. A few minutes later, the same hand is laid on a scanner: at the police station we get fingerprinted and detained. We are failed asylum seekers.

Some twenty migrants, including me, are taken to the airport. We fly to Milan. Italy is 'my' country, according to the Dublin agreement. Once we land, we are again with the police: fingerprinting, deportation order, detention, over and over. I am really getting sick of it. I have learnt to be patient, but this is turning into a nightmare. I am twenty-four years old.

An Embassy

What am I doing in this elegant room? A group of policemen surround me in a weird atmosphere. A smiling and smart Somali man is patting my shoulder – 'Behave, my boy, behave' – before he hands a policeman a sheet with the Somali Embassy heading. I was told this was a place of misery, fraud and bribery. It seems everything has changed, at least on the surface. In a few moments, the policemen and I are back in the car. They handcuff me until we get to the airport in Rome and on the plane my wrists are freed.

Claiming I wanted to go back to Somalia was simply a strategy. I could take no more of detention and isolation. It didn't work, though. I could not imagine that they would actually arrange my deportation to a war-torn country so quickly. I called the Ombudsman, the lawyer, UNHCR. The return procedure got suspended, but I'm still stuck in the camp.

And something strange just happened. Two guards passed by; one was speaking to the other, while staring at me. He wanted me to listen. He was repeating things I had mentioned in my private calls from here. How is he aware? He wants me to know that they know. This is a mouse-trap.

An Ending

What am I doing in this country? Have I ever considered moving somewhere else? Of course I have. But I know that a different state – France, for instance – could easily reject me and send me back here. And moving would also mean starting from the beginning, once again. After the conviction, they say you are always monitored, for the next five years at least. I heard it on TV and from people in prison. In such circumstances it would be difficult to build something new. People may feel scared to know someone like me. It is not easy living like this.

Finally, my last request for asylum has been accepted. I can move as a free man in this country. I have got mixed feelings about Italy, though. People are very different from those in Northern Europe; they talk a lot and are more social. I am not, but I have got friends. Italy did something unjust to me, the judge knows it, but I am giving it a chance. I am currently studying to get my driving licence and will soon learn how to flow through such tiny, twisting streets.

The Outsider's Tale

as told to

Bidisha

EVEN MY HOME COUNTRY wasn't home. In the place I grew up, I was invisible, as I am now. Our people were stateless even there. All I knew from childhood was being hated – hated so I could not attend school, hated so I could not attend college, hated and prevented from getting a job, hated and denied access to the hospital. Just because of my heritage. The only work we could get earned us barely enough to eat, nowhere near enough to improve ourselves. My father and I washed cars in the car park of the supermarket for coins, nothing more.

We protested in the streets for our human rights. My father was first in line. He stood up and said, 'I want to talk about freedom for our people,' but got no further before the police turned the water cannons on us. We lay sprawling, battered by the bruising water and unable to breathe. Then they trampled through us, beating us with their batons.

I got to my feet and dozens of us ran together, a crowd of strangers. I heard someone breathing heavily behind me. I turned to look and it was a policeman. He hit me in the face. I was too dazed to fight. He and another policeman dragged me into their car, which sped away in a cloud of dust. Every time I raised my head to look out, they pushed it down again. All I know is they drove for a long time.

They took me to a special police compound and kept me there for two months. Every other night they pulled me out, beat me up, shouted, beat me up, shouted; a different assailant every time, and just when I thought the beating was finished, it'd start again. After two months of that, they shoved me out, took my fingerprints and told me I had to become an informant, or else. If you refuse, you're against the government, you're against the security forces, you're against the royal family, you're dead.

They handcuffed and blindfolded me, put me in a car, drove for hours and then dumped me on the street. When I finally got home, everything about me was tired. My chest, my knees, my legs. All I wanted was to rest. I got two days of it before they were back at the door. They pushed their way inside, showed me photographs of people who'd been protesting alongside me and my father, and asked, 'Where are they? Where can we find them?'

When they were gone, my mother and I talked long into the night. The people in the photographs had families, they had children. They weren't nameless or faceless to those who loved them. I wouldn't inform on them. After all, they were innocent.

★

I left the country after a long night hiding on a farm in the middle of nowhere, my new passport getting sweaty in my palm. A week after that, the police went to my house, ransacked it and threatened my parents.

Thus began my odyssey of being faceless in nameless places and nameless in faceless places, in the company of strangers from all over the world, all refugees like me. I went to one country – I don't know which one, I didn't yet speak English – then to Turkey, then to Greece. In every place, we met a man who passed us on to the next place. Greece was the worst. We stayed a month, maybe two, in an apartment owned by a man who tried to use us as slaves, shunting us to different properties to clean them. He beat us and threatened us until we did it. The most disturbing thing was the way he was so nice and polite to other people.

Then there were more countries whose names I didn't know, and then in Belgium I encountered a dilemma. If I registered as being from my home country, they would let my country's government know – the same people who'd threatened me with death if I didn't become an informant. I told this to the guy in Belgium and he shrugged, 'Just register as Iraqi.' Am I Iraqi? Have I even been to Iraq? Do I know anything about Iraq? No, no and no. I went from being faceless, nameless and placeless to almost being an actual fake person, a pretend Iraqi.

North Belgium was my lowest point. The locals hated us there, hated and abused us. Finally, I found myself in Brussels, homeless. I was so tired that one day I entered a mosque in the city and spilled my guts to the imam there, and to my surprise, he knew everything about my people. He brought me food, he told me not to worry, he said there were people I could talk to and a place I could go. It was a Friday – that's how clearly I remember it.

*

We'd been in the boat for nearly eight hours when the British police picked us up – but not before we'd been rammed by another, bigger boat and caught on the coast guard's radar. Me and dozens of others in life vests, terrified of drowning. I'd been thrown into the boat by a strange guy in Calais, who started off angrily ordering us about, but when that didn't work he suddenly became nice and kind and polite. I know money changed hands to get me there, but I never saw it.

Once we were on dry land, I heard English and other languages. I was too tired to sleep, but I was happy. We arrived at Dover at three in the morning. They called our names, took us to the processing centre, we had showers and food and everything. Not everyone spoke well to us, I'll say that, and they fingerprinted us at that first interview. Then it was a series of chain hotels in North London – two months in Brent Cross, two months in Wembley. By now my language skills made me the unofficial interpreter between the refugees and the hotel managers, the night staff, the day staff. I still got put through the system like everyone else: Migrant Help, processing, orientation, integration. Pulled out of one hotel at 7am and transferred to an immigration removal centre, the manager at the old centre crying because he was going to miss me, telling the taxi driver I'm a good guy.

At the immigration removal centre, I knew I was near the airport because I could hear the planes landing and taking off. They took everything out of my pockets, I waited for an hour and then I had an interview with a very nice young woman. I told her everything and I told her the truth. And then I went back to another detention centre for two weeks. Time passed under constant tension: I did my English courses, exercised, got a phone, helped everyone translate. But the tension never let up. I had removal directions five days from when I arrived in one centre and it wasn't until day four that it was cancelled. The stress was incredible – the worry, and the frustration and anger from the poor guidance I received from the legal firms. I talked to a lawyer who couldn't accept my case but gave me 'advice'. The second lawyer did the same thing. The third lawyer kept me waiting for three hours then did the same thing. I was told by people to make a fuss when they tried to deport me – to make some noise and say that I wasn't safe if they sent me on.

By the time I got a proper solicitor who actually talked to me for several hours, two of my friends in the same position had attempted suicide.

★

Now I'm careful as I wait. I ask politely for my towel because my skin is very sensitive and it reacts to everything. I eat the brown, soggy food they give us in plastic containers from a company called Treats. When one of the guys here is angry or frustrated, I take him downstairs and interpret for him. Not all of them are good guys – you see, when you translate for someone you see what they do and what they're like. At my Home Office meetings, I never get angry. I don't shout or hit the table. I say, 'Okay, thank you, very kind.' I tell them everything about being nameless and faceless in my 'home' country – and in all the countries in between. I've now been at the same hotel since last summer and I'm still waiting in limbo. The coronavirus has made it all so much more frightening – being held in a hotel during a pandemic that's killing so many people, unseen, unnamed, unnoticed and unprotected. When I translate and interpret for others, I try to do it without sitting close to anyone and I use sanitiser on my hands every time I touch a door handle. But it's difficult, and scary.

I just want to live and work, as people here do. I am waiting for another interview.

I have a little contact with my family, but I don't tell them anything that would make them sad.

The Waiting Man's Tale

as told to

Rachel Seiffert

I'VE BEEN THROUGH SO much. So much.

These are not just words. I hear it in your voice; I see it in your face too, when the video call connects.

But then you smile a moment.

We both do: me, before my laptop; you, with your phone screen in hand. We nod our grateful hellos, glad that we can speak across the miles like this, make contact in this strange pandemic time marked by distance, by separation. I am locked down in London, you in the northern town where the Home Office has placed you.

But as soon as I ask, *how have you been keeping?* your smile goes again; you look to the window.

– I've been through so much. So much. And now I am stuck, you know? I am really stuck here. Waiting.

You are far from your family. Your two sisters, your nieces and nephews scattered across London. For twenty years – ever since you were a boy still – the city has been home to you. Brixton, Peckham, Lewisham: the same south-of-the-river places I call home as well.

Life here goes on, even in these plague days. There is school for the young, work for me, and for your sisters. I could visit them – even now. I could walk to one, take a bus to the other;

I could knock at either of their front doors, stand on their front steps and talk. For you, though, this is near-on impossible. Financially, logistically. And you fear the rules might change. *The rules, the rules.* You fear you might fall foul of them, *without even knowing.*

Experience has made you cautious: you know that – for someone in your shoes – there are always consequences.

– I just have to wait.

You shrug into the phone camera: what else can you do?

It is not right, though, I reply, that you must wait so far away. But you insist now:

– It is OK, it is OK.

You wave a palm; you don't want to dwell on this.

– Let us not dwell on sadness. I do not want to think too much about that.

Instead, you take me on a small tour of the house you have been placed in. The video jumps and stutters as you stand up, carrying your phone from the shared living room to the narrow kitchen.

– Say hello to the kettle.

You laugh.

– Here is the toaster.

You turn the screen to show me: all the nooks and all the corners.

– And here, here is my cooker. You see now?

You see the funny side, giggling at how you have to squash yourself against the fridge door so that I can see both you and it at the same time – so we can share a smile.

It all looks really nice! I say. Because it does: the house is cosy, orderly. So I am relieved, too: it is not a bad house to be stuck in. To wait in.

You have told me about your housemates – *my colleagues,* you call them – and they sound like good people to be stuck with. *We are in the same boat; we are here as one family.* The three men you share with, they have all been in your shoes: waiting for their

ID cards, for their 'leave to remain'. Should yours come through now, I imagine it would feel more like a 'leave to leave', or a 'leave to return' to London, to your family, and that would be so very welcome. But I do not say this out loud; I know you do not want to dwell. And I see you have more to show me as well.

– Wait! Did I say yet? We have a garden!

Holding your phone out in front of you, you open the back door, stepping me into the sudden flare of outside.

The day is bright cold, the sky blue as blue. Over the low back wall, you show me the houses opposite: a northern town street, two-up-two-down terraces, with front doors opening onto the pavement. Turning your phone to one side, you reveal a run of small back yards just like yours: brick walls, brick underfoot, empty washing lines strung at head height.

You tilt the phone upwards – to the sky, and the telephone wires running high and for miles. You point to their tramlines against the bright blue; and then you turn me to face the horizon, to the hills rising there.

– You see them?

I do.

– They are beautiful.

They are. And I am glad that you enjoy them; that you turn your phone so I can see how you grin in the sunlight.

The town, though; I know it is in a valley. *A dark one*, you have told me.

Furthermore, you have been placed there; it is not your place.

And as though this isn't enough, you are reminded – too often, by others – that you are out of place there. By the old man spitting on the pavement as you pass. By the youths who ask, *what you doing here, Black man?*

Stepping back inside now, your smile fades again as you tell me:

– At times. At times, I feel I am waiting in the shadow of the valley of death – you know?

Again, you look to the window.

So in the quiet that follows, I ask:

Tell me, G. What was before this?

I know you were in London. Close to family, to familiarity, community; all that brings ease – even though London life hasn't always been easy.

But before we talk of that part, we go back further, into Ghana childhood days. To Asante province, where you were born, and where you lived your boyhood; where you had family around you also.

– I had my grandmother, my aunties.

You count them on your fingers.

– My cousins and uncles.

School filled your mornings; the mile and a half walk there and back with the other boys. After lessons, you went to your uncle's farm, where you tended the plantain, the cassava.

But you have been through so much – *so much* – I remind myself. I know you left Ghana for good reason, so I am braced to hear more. Still, what you tell me next, it takes me aback.

– From my home, I was kidnapped.

You close your eyes.

– I was taken.

A local feud turning violent, a local dispute spilling out beyond all reason, you were caught up in its turmoil – and you were just a boy still.

– I was beaten. I was held. I think it was for weeks; it might have been for months.

The confusion of that time shows in your features, in the way you pass your hand across your forehead, uneasy with recalling, with retelling what was so hard.

You were released – eventually – back to your family. But they were still frightened; they had lost trust in the authorities. So they decided, better you go to Accra. Even better: you go to London. Make the Mother Country journey, the one your sisters had already made before you. They both had their British passports; in time, you would be able to get yours; and there, with them, you would have security.

For a while, that was what you had.

You came on a visa to finish your schooling. You stayed on and worked: in supermarket warehouses first, then painting and decorating, maintaining council houses for various borough authorities.

But the Mother Country turned hostile in the meanwhile.

Demands for paperwork started, for documents and evidence. *The rules, the rules*: this was the first time you fell foul of them. You were told you had overstayed your visa; you were told you had overstayed your welcome.

And now you pause a while in our conversation, looking away from the phone, turning to the window; thinking, frowning: how to say all this?

You do not want to make excuses.

You know your family should have got your papers in order, that you should have applied earlier for your British passport, to become a British citizen. But you do want to explain to me, how it is, when you find yourself in this situation: young and unwelcome, and on the wrong side of the law.

It hurts, you say, in a way that turns you.

It changes you, in ways you would not think possible.

– If you are not someone who uses drugs, you might end up using drugs. Things you think you would not do, you will end up doing.

This is what experience has taught you. Because you ended up using, you ended up selling.

– And so then, one year and ten months, I was in prison.

We sit quietly for a while after you say this. Your story is hard to tell – there is *so much* you have been through; such experiences. The kind that overwhelm, the sort that would mark anyone, even the strongest.

But you tell me prison was not the hardest.

– No! Prison was a chance for me.

You say this with emphasis.

And then you explain:

– I could work again.

You could think and talk through your experiences; you could help others.

– I could be active. Active, you know? I felt I could make a change in life.

But when you were released this time – eventually – it was not to your family.

Stepping out of the prison gates, there was a deportation team waiting; you were taken straight from prison to Home Office detention.

– This, you see? This is when my waiting started.

You tell me of the room without windows you had to sleep in; the terrible uncertainty; the back and forth with the authorities; the long meetings and telephone calls, exchanges with lawyers, who come and go, come and go.

– Another one year and ten months I served there. Another one year and ten months, on top of my sentence. The first one was for a crime. But the second? What had I done?

You should never have been kept for so long.

Even now, detention haunts you. The thought of being taken back there; that such an order might come for you, any moment, in a letter, a phone call.

– Night is a struggle. I have to tell you.

You shake your head.

– I am scared right now. I am really scared.

Just this morning, a letter came, unexpected, from the Home Office. Not a deportation notice – thanks be – but still, it has set off your anxiety.

– It's about my benefits. There was an overpayment.

It is a demand for money, for documents – neither of which you have, of course. How can you work without papers? How can you have money without work? This is the never-ending cycle you are caught in. This is how your life turns while you are waiting. And you have no lawyer to help you at the moment.

– What do I say this time?

You look at me, on your phone screen, and then at the paper, passing a hand across your face once more.

– I told the Home Office already: take five pounds each week from my allowance. I can manage that.

Five pounds from your weekly 39? I am horrified: those are cut-to-the-bone calculations.

You nod, slow, and then you lift the letter to show me:

– But here, look: they say I must pay seven pounds.

And the way you say this – *se-ven-pounds* – all the syllables counted out – it has me wondering: is that the difference, perhaps, between eating tomorrow or not?

This is what waiting is. This is what waiting does.

For a while we talk about lawyers; about next steps, about sorting out this letter mess. Most likely it's been spat out by a Home Office computer, issued according to a pre-ordained schedule; a standard demand for all those whose benefits have been miscalculated. It will have nothing to do with your 'leave to remain' decision. But still. It leaves you to explain what should not need explaining. It leaves you feeling precarious.

I am scared right now, I am really scared.

A moment later, though, you breathe in, breathe out; you calm yourself. And when you speak again, your voice is stronger:

– I have to live in the day to day.

This is what you have learned is best.

– I find some small things to be glad of each morning. Even just some small thing – it can help me.

You look around yourself, to find me an example.

– So, this evening – maybe I will cook a piece of chicken.

You give a little laugh. A little wry. And you look to the

window; again, you look to the window – but you do not let your smile fade this time.

Instead, you hold up a mug that has been sitting next to you as we talk.

– See? You see this? I will make a cuppa. I think now I will make myself a hot chocolate.

We end our call on that note. Not dwelling on sadness; finding ways to look forwards, even if they have to be small ones at the moment.

But I want to pass this on now – all that you have said to me.

How hard the wait is.

The *so much* you have been through.

And what it takes to live each day as you do.

Night is a struggle, I have to tell you.
But each time morning comes, I am glad again.
And I am waiting. I am waiting.

The Poet's Tale

as told by

Kyon Ferril

CANADA ATTEMPTS TO DENY the fact that it employs a system of indefinite immigration detention by leaning on semantics: because every detainee is eligible for a monthly detention review, no one is technically detained for more than one month at a time. By some strange and self-serving logic, the indefiniteness of these monthly instalments is not taken into consideration. Enter Kyon Ferril, whose story stands as a condemnation of this contradictory and inhumane system. In over three years in immigration detention, Kyon faced some 40 such detention reviews, often overseen by the same adjudicator of the Immigration and Refugee Board, and often lasting only a few minutes before he was remanded to a further month's detention.

The fact that we can read the poems gathered here, and – perhaps even more importantly – hear his resistant voice, is testament to both the human spirit, and to Kyon's own indomitable will to be free, to be heard, and to live a meaningful life. These poems were mostly written while Kyon was held as a migrant detainee in Central East Correctional Centre, a maximum-security prison in Lindsay, Ontario. Their author was born in Jamaica and came to Canada as a four-year-old child, growing up in West End Toronto, where he loved to garden with his Ma and try different cuisines. He has spent the better part of his young adulthood – from his late teens to his late twenties – navigating the discriminatory system of double punishment and immigration detention. While detained, Kyon has been an active organiser for the rights of prisoners and detained persons, to the point of suffering for his outspokenness in the form of physical violence, extended prison sentences, and transfer to higher level security facilities. Kyon writes that he 'is intent and focused on rebuilding his life and his broader community through poetry. His creative contribution to society is to help remember the voiceless or those made voiceless on the grounds of class, race, sexuality or citizenship. He takes up this work at a critical level, streaming from within his self and through external reflection regarding his dual carceral status of inhumane arbitrary detention.'

– Stephen Collis, Erin Goheen Glanville & Ayendri Riddell

Come down from there

COME DOWN FROM THERE, you can't keep that to yourself,
  your heart, isn't meant for a shelf, for there's other hearts
another heart just for you.

But what about that other heart watching my heart for a
  sign, from the other shelf in the shadow.

Was my placement, my heart, truly alone?
  I can't keep my heart to myself, but whose is it I shall share
this heart with (confusion), care for, be there for,

For once attached where you go I'll follow, as an individual
heart I'm worried to call another heart home.

Heart Castaway

My heart's walking away, heavy way down, weighted down
  inflamed within melted compound from what it's been abused
and used, too (without a compass) along the long road back
                                        for acceptance
  through the highway of pain.

For what is real, is fake, what is good never existed in the
                                        highway.
  All is distorted like time which leaves and never returns.
This heart longs for more… time,
  that evaporates for it does not reside in the highway of pain.

Nothing past resembles tomorrow, what was, will never be the
  same. So I continue walking on, in and without (a compass)
through the highway of pain.

This heart searches for acceptance in society, from its family
  and from itself, while detained and segregated in the highway
of pain.

This heart is forever labelled a foreign national
  is any of this heart's pain foreign?

This heart, my heart, is a citizen of pain.

Central East Correctional Centre, January 15, 2015, Artspace

How can I complain against or fight against a system
   I'm fighting to be a part of. Am I not legitimising
the perpetration and separation of an unjust systematic
   oppression, that humiliates and strips individuals of their
dignity. Is this a fight I want to continue?

   Significantly my heart has been reduced to one of not
my own, its substance corralled and leveraged to prey upon
   society's innocence, an innocence that's hungry to become
mature.

How do you establish maturity while perpetually
   confined, every carbon footprint rendered from your
being. We are educated as individuals but suffer under
   deplorable conditions in masses.

For I do not benefit from oppression, this is true, we do
   not benefit from oppression, but without, knowledge
how does an individual know when and if they're being
   oppressed?

Eat knowledge, to eat the oppressor.

Oppress no more!

Memory is an individual's greatest weapon

Memory is an individual's greatest weapon. Memories are a
   personal and unique component to life as our thoughts travel
through realms of one memory plane of a despairful event, it's
   fundamentally expressed, our environment shapes us. I greatly
empathise it's our recollection of events that compounds and
tailors an individual's environment for memories.

Your memory is a weapon consistently deployed against you,
                                          a weapon
   consistently deployed against the private and public sectors,
against immigrants who make up and are comprised of these
                                          sectors,
   against immigrants and detainees who bleed through their
labour to manufacture these sectors.

Our memories are preyed upon and reshaped for political
gain through resentment, exploitation, extraction and
                              displacement,
   'cause our memories are fickle (excuse) it's socially easier
to digest institutional thought than to challenge and deconstruct
   the systemic views intended for thought.

As humans our memories are our greatest asset of mass
destruction, for they build us and break us down and amplify
   through the night, when isolated and confined to a realm,
a space composed of solid material (steel an' concrete), this is not
   a memory, this is my reality, detained I am.

What does your memory mean to you when it is not your
own, 'cause you cannot remember?

For every memory is the same: concrete.

The system will break your heart

The system will break your heart, if you pledge absolute
                                        belief and trust
in administrators, its gate keepers, only to become astonished
by what lies within: broken men, vulnerable hearts, valuable
to the system's function, lives rendered unvaluable, worthless

Set and established (enshrined) by pre-conceived conditions:
                                                    wealth,
power, control. Don't let it break your heart, the truth will
do it. Do your research and evident is the shapeshifting qualities
of administrators, but the gears / mechanism of institutional
                                            obfuscation
remains or is concrete.

I am ignored and detained throughout this process.

Hope is knowledge

Hope is knowledge and is attainable in darkness, in our
darkest hour it's translucent and transparent, but visible under
all conditions through an individual's will.

Hope has moving characteristics that can create or extinguish
life for it's an interchangeable life force, unique and touchable
in all elements, hope is only lost when our environment
overcomes and shifts our focus from our being.

Focus and will are necessary ingredients to capture.
As we evolve, so too does our hope. Hope is alive,
it lives, it lingers everywhere, taste it, for it's on our tongues,
in our words in our eyes behind every shade (orange) of our skies.
Hope lives. Hope is an entity commodified in cycles yet gifted
in promises. Hope transforms the dull and ungifted.

Hope is humility and restraint, hope is what Dickinson's message
means to me, that continuously resonates and is lifted in
the wind, tainted in laughter and sorrow; moulded in sand or
clay, in everything (we touch) or our flesh encounters.

Hope is like a fragrance, it's sweet as an ocean's mist,
hope floods our chromosomes like high tides, it laps at our feet,
it finds and guides us as we wander aimlessly to its
savory aromas, forever embedded and married to our engine,
our hearts.

This is my creation of hope that's alive and well, I hope for us
all, this is my hope for you…

How do we establish equality within individual countries, within
boundaries, when equality is captured and limited? Is equality
not borderless and a universal essential essence to life?

Hope is reachable like a goal, for hope is pinchable through will. I hope for greater equality, for equality equals balance.

I continue to hope... I hope... to hope on...

The Stowaway's Tale

as told to

Amy Sackville

SOMETHING HAPPENS, SOMETHING VIOLENT, and you have to leave your home. You have no ties to keep you, nothing left to leave behind. You sneak on board a ship, a ship to anywhere but here, to a place where you think you might find a new start, and prosper. Your life has not been full of opportunity, so you take this one. You hide below decks until your hunger drives you out of your hiding place and you are discovered by the crew. The captain of the ship is kind to you. You arrive in a new country. You are a young man in search of a better life.

This is something like your story. This is the familiar shape of the stowaway's tale: a story about pluck and prospect, full of risk and daring and charm. But that's not your story, not quite.

You are a young man, in your twenties. At home, you worked as a kind of porter, you helped people carry things and they paid you what they could afford. This was the kind of work available. Certainly not much in the way of opportunity. But then something happened and you had to run, you had to get on a ship and leave. You don't want me to write about the particular, unspeakable thing that happened to you and your family and your home, the thing that you ran from. So all I will say is that it was brutal and quick and confusing, that you escaped, and that you believe now that your family are dead. I ask if you have heard anything from home, since you arrived in the UK. Who am I going to call? you ask. I opened our conversation by apologising in advance for any stupid or tactless questions. You don't know anyone from home, now. You don't have any more family. When you ran away you waited for them at the port, you waited for news, and when the news came and it was bad, you knew you had to go. You tell me the story quietly, flatly. You tell me you have nightmares, you have flashbacks, that this is what you see when you're sleeping and when you can't sleep.

When we first speak, this is what you describe – the thing I won't describe here, the violent thing that happened. It's early in 2021 and we are speaking through a screen, of course. I am in my home with all my stuff around me and you are speaking from a plain white room, the only feature of which I can see is the line between the wall and the ceiling behind your head. I listen, and I don't know what to say; the usual platitudes for loss will not apply here. I think I say I can't imagine what that's like. Well, but that doesn't help you, does it.

The second time we speak, I ask you more about the journey, your journey as a stowaway. I realise that I have been picturing a small craft, possibly rigged and made of wood; you told me you'd found a small hiding place and I'm picturing some below-deck hold to curl up in. This is just the image that arrives in my head, vaguely historical, eighteenth century. I don't really think that this is what it was like. People arrive this way, stowed away in boats, of course; it's on the news. I know this. But I have not imagined what that's like, have not known how to imagine it, the space or the time of it. I ask you to tell me. It's an ugly, frightening story and there is nothing romantic about it.

So once you had waited for weeks at the port, and none of your family had turned up – once you had heard that they weren't going to – then you knew you had to leave, and you found a fisherman who would take you to a ship. You helped him with his fishing and then he brought you close to what I now understand was a huge container ship. You didn't care where it was going to take you as long as it was Europe, because you thought you would be safe there; and you knew this ship brought cars to your country, and you thought: all ships that bring cars, they all go to Europe. You climb onto the ship, a docking bay at the back. At the back of the ship, there are boxes, things that look like a box, you explain. There are *loads* of them. Now I can see it: one of those impossibly massive ships stacked with crates and crates in different dirty colours, that can be seen off the coast of Kent. And when you are inside one of the boxes, no one can see you from outside. When you got on board you found some other stowaways there already, and you each had your own box. You had a few biscuits and a plastic bottle of water for the journey. You didn't know how long it would be, since you didn't know where you were going. You stayed in this thing like a box for eight or nine days, you think. I ask how it felt, being in the box. It is what it is, you say. You didn't care about the days; you didn't know how many had passed until you arrived in England. You just wanted to get far away.

The thing that looks like a box is not that wide, to sleep in. You can only sleep on your side. And so you sometimes leave the box and talk to the other people there. And if you need the toilet you go down to a small place, you say, and you grab onto something so you don't fall overboard. One night, you hear a shout, and you realise that someone is missing. The thing he was holding wasn't strong enough. You and the others try to open the door to the deck, then, to get help from the crew, but it's locked. Later, another night, you are hungry – of course you are hungry – and you try the door again and this time you manage to force the lock. You're hungry and one of you has fallen overboard and you're realising you will have to get out of this space to survive. You and another stowaway go to look for food in the kitchen and this is when they find you.

At first, the captain and the crew are nice to you. It's the captain who advises you that when you put into port, you should seek asylum. You didn't know this word. They put you and the others in a cabin, and they lock it, but they give you food and are nice to you. But then things change; something seems wrong. The captain has been in contact with the company that owns the ship, and the company wants to send you back home. Now the crew leave food for you at the window when you're asleep and it's cold by the time you wake up. *Cold*, you say. By which I think you mean frozen – this is winter, and it was a very cold winter. Something is not right and you're scared now, scared you'll be taken back home. The window of the cabin is welded with an iron bar, and someone manages to pull the bar free and you all climb out and find somewhere else to hide.

When the crew find you they have weapons, you say. Metal poles. You and your friends take the bars that were used to bar the doors, to scare them away you say, just to leave us alone. The crew retreats; the captain keeps telling you to get back in the cabin but you know that they will lock you in more securely this time and take you back and you refuse. You stay outside that December night; you take it in turns to sit in a bathroom for warmth. Then the authorities come, and they put you in handcuffs and you're in port by now, you are in the UK, and the police say come down, you're okay. It's a weekend, and you sleep at the police station until Monday. And on Monday you're taken to court. Court for what? you ask. There are charges against you. Affray. At the court, they say this case can't be dealt with in this court. And you are taken away again, and this time they take you to prison. A week later this process is repeated: to court; this case can't be dealt with in this court; back to a different prison. You are bewildered – as you're telling me, you're bewildered. You didn't know what 'affray' is, you'd never heard that kind of word before. I was trying to have a conversation with the captain, you say. I didn't threaten anybody, I didn't threaten anyone – so why are we going to court? From that day I arrived, you say, I don't know what's going on.

You keep coming back to it: how you arrived and you went straight to prison. You can't process it. In fact, it's the very first thing you said to me, when I asked why you wanted to share your story. You said: Because I don't see the point, if someone is coming here from another country, seeking for asylum, and the same day is sent to prison. You repeat this phrase a few times: I don't see the point. There is a kind of exasperation, bafflement, that comes into your voice. Rhetorical questions. You shake your head in disbelief. When you were in prison, waiting for trial, the solicitor told you not to worry, it's going to be over. It's going to be over?! It took *months*. You rub your eyes as you speak, and I think you are very tired. You have nightmares, you have flashbacks. You tell me: The thing that I'm trying to say is, if people run away from their country, they don't run away for no reason. And if they run away for a reason, I don't see the point why immigration can't help them. You expected detention; you expected a slow process. You didn't expect to go to prison. You tell me: If I'd had a sign from my country that this was going to happen, I'm not going to get on the ship. I'm just going to die in my country. Yeah. I'm just going to stay there and die.

You were in prison for ten months before trial. During this time, you felt you had been forgotten. That no one cared about you, or even knew about you. An immigration officer came to interview you, and they brought you a paper to sign to say you wanted to go back to your country. You say, I wasn't in my senses, I was stressed, I was depressed. So I said there's no point. That they *should* send me back, let me go back to my own country and die if that's the case. You signed the paper. But here, a stranger's kindness intervened: another prisoner noticed that you were not in a fit state, not in your own senses. And you were seen by a doctor and given medication and your claim was renewed.

You went to another prison, a third prison, for the duration of the trial, which was two months. The charges make no sense to you. You are, again, animated by the absurdity of them. How would we get a knife? How did we hijack the ship? You are cleared of some, but not all of the charges. By the time you received your sentence, you had been in prison so long that you had only a few months left to serve. And when those months were over, the day your sentence was finished, you were packed and ready to go, to be taken into detention. What had you packed? I ask. What were your possessions? This is another of the stupid questions I warned you I might ask. My clothes, you say shortly. You have brought nothing with you. Just the clothes you have from prison, in your bag. The day comes and goes. What's going on? You're told you're being held under immigration laws. They say it's up to them when you're let out of prison. Whenever they're ready. Almost a month later you are released into detention.

In the detention centre, it's a little better. You have some space to yourself, after months of sharing rooms with strangers. You can move around, exercise for more than 45 minutes a day. You have things to do: you serve food to the other detainees, you clean. It takes your mind off things. But you can't sleep. You see a doctor. He gives you medication for one week. He doesn't tell you it is just for a week. When you ask for more, you are told you can't have these drugs for more than a week. At this time, you are sleeping less than 30 minutes, 25 minutes, you say, that's the whole of my sleep. You are having nightmares, flashbacks. The things you saw at home and the things you've seen in prison. These things keep coming into your head all the time, and you don't know how to make it stop. You have harmed yourself. Two times, you tried to kill yourself. So there's nothing I can do, you say, I just keep bearing the pain like that until I got out of detention. You look at the camera, at me, for a long moment and I don't know what to say, and you look away.

You came here for a better life, in a safe place. Now you are waiting. You live in a house that the Home Office put you in and there's not much to do. We're in lockdown now, of course, but I don't think it makes much difference, except that the gym is closed; you can't work, anyway, though you would like to, and you don't have much to live on, only what you're given. You work out, clean your room. You skip meals so you have a little more to spend. If you can stay, if your claim is approved, then you can finish your schooling. You tell me: I do have a plan – if I can start working, anybody that needs help, if I'm in a position to help them then I'm going to help them. Because the way I see people, suffering, I don't like it. But I'm not in a good position to help them.

You have been changed by what's happened to you. Now, you don't feel yourself; you don't do things correctly, you say. You find it hard to concentrate. There are two other people in the house you live in and you talk to them sometimes, but sometimes, you tell me, I just lock my door, stay inside. I know it's not supposed to be like that.

I'm not going to lie, the prison and the detention has fucked my head up, because I don't think I'm going to be normal for years, you say. This is the only time you swear and you say it very softly. But the way I am now – there's something wrong with me in my head, because sometimes I do harm myself, sometimes I do try and kill myself because when I have those nightmares… the things I've seen in prison… honestly I do see them, and I do have nightmares of those things. And I'm not supposed to go to prison, I don't know why they took me to prison. I know, people that have been sent back, they've been killed. If I know they're going to send me back, I don't know what's going to happen. Because I'm not going to go back. One day they might find my dead body in the house. That's it. I'm not going to lie.

This is another phrase that you use – I'm not going to lie – and it's idiomatic and when you say it, you sound like any other young man but you also sound like you mean it, you need to be believed, and I do believe you.

As we come to the end of our conversation, your housemate keeps calling for you and you shout that you're coming, you're on the phone, and you smile and shake your head. I ask if there's anything you wanted to ask me. You laugh and tell me that if I was from the government you'd have *loads* of questions to ask me. What would you ask? You say, anyone that came to this country, they came for a reason. They should be given a chance. You tell me: The important part of my story is that when people leave their country, they come to this country, they're not supposed to be sent to prison. Most people, they don't have enough strength to cope. It shouldn't be like that. Because those things, they do cost, to a human being.

The Activist's Tale

as told to
Dina Nayeri

Twenty years ago, Solomon's father vanished into a Guinean police station.

Solomon watched his Baba, flanked by five military officers, walk away for the last time, fatigue slowing his gait, slackening his jaw beneath his blindfold. The officers had come to the family farm late at night, in a tinted-glass Land Rover. Solomon's father, Alpha, rose from his sleep to answer the door. The men pushed their way in, covered Alpha's eyes, and handcuffed Solomon. They dragged the two men out of the house, tossed them in the back of the vehicle, and sped away from the family's compound. The roads were rough, winding, and dark, the neighbours asleep. How strange that they should blindfold Baba, and only Baba, as if to inflict this indignity on a respected Fula elder.

In the morning, they released Solomon, ordering him to report to the station once a week. 'And Baba?' he wanted to ask, but what was the point? For an hour he walked toward home, no money in his pocket for food or bus fare. He passed the time fretting, counting his steps. What happens now. What will happen next time? Where is Baba? After the other arrests, they had been released together. But to disappear, blindfolded, with military police into the deeper parts of the station meant only this: his Baba had been taken away to die.

An hour is a long time to wonder, mouth dry and belly

rumbling, about what home will look like when you get there – will the children be playing among the kola trees? Will his wife be making lunch, or will she be crying in the bedroom? Will she be gone too? It's a long time to think back on all the ways *this* terrifying incident is different from all the *other* terrifying incidents. Baba had been arrested seven times before. After every release, he became involved in the Fula opposition again, and so Solomon, his eldest child, did too.

★

Solomon was born in Hérico, a village in the Labé region of Northern Guinea. His parents were both Fula people, a long oppressed ethnic minority who practice Islam and are scattered across West Africa. They had met because his father, a farmer, was exporting kola nuts to the markets in Gambia, where his mother traded palm oil and fresh vegetables. As a boy, Solomon studied in English in Gambia, because his mother thought it would give him more opportunities than the French his sisters had learned. When he finished his studies, he returned to the farm in Hérico. His father was now an anti–regime activist, and young Solomon wanted to help. Together Solomon and Alpha organised a youth group for the Fula opposition party against the military Junta and its autocratic leader, President Lansana Conté.

After every campaign, father and son were arrested, held for a few days in police custody, unceremoniously released, then tossed into prison again. Each time, they returned to the farm with its many trees, they gathered kola nuts in the rainy season and tended to the trees in the dry season, worked in the small supermarket that Alpha owned, and, alongside this, they staged more campaigns. They survived this way for a decade. Amid the unrest, Solomon married and had two sons.

His mother, afraid for their lives, escaped with his younger sisters to Gambia. But his father insisted that Solomon stay on the farm, to fight and to work. 'Go with the girls,' he told his wife. 'Leave Solomon here to be a man.' So, Solomon said goodbye to his mother, to a home filled with the smell of her domoda stew with just the right portion of ground nut, her fried chicken, her benachin, and her okra soup.

Now, Baba was gone. No one tried to say that he was alive. And one night soon, the men might return for Solomon. The worst crimes, Solomon now understood, were committed under the cover of law.

Baba's friend, a lorry driver between Gambia and Guinea, came to Solomon one night. 'You have to go,' he said. 'I'll take you in my truck.'

A few days later, Solomon kissed his family goodbye and climbed into the covered back of the lorry. His father's friend would drive him most of the way to Gambia, where his mother and sisters were waiting. The friend gave him food and money. He called Solomon's mother and said 'Solomon is on his way.'

The journey in the back of the lorry took three days. Solomon stayed under cover, so that the hours melted together. He didn't see the Guinean sun again. Over the border with Senegal, he kept hidden, his breath the only sound. When the lorry had cleared the checkpoint, his friend found a quiet spot and left him to make his own way through Senegal. From there, Solomon took trains and buses deeper into Senegal, and crossed into Gambia on foot.

For a few months he stayed with his mother and tried to make plans. 'I have to escape from Africa,' he told her. 'I have to go to Europe, to save my life. Gambia isn't safe.' Gambia too was under military rule; and President Jammeh was even more notorious than Conté with a paramilitary unit that committed human rights abuses with impunity. If he drew their attention, Solomon could easily be returned to Guinea.

A few weeks later, a childhood friend sent Solomon his own European passport to use in his escape, since he wasn't eligible for a Gambian one, and didn't want to alert the Guinean authorities to his whereabouts. 'Come to Europe where it's safe,' he said.

'You should go,' his mother said. 'This is why you learned English. Go. Live a good life.'

Solomon's maternal uncle had a friend in the Gambian airport, an immigration officer, who wouldn't look too closely at the photo in Solomon's passport. There was a direct flight to the United Kingdom. This was his one chance for the kind of life his mother had wanted for him.

Solomon knew nothing about asylum, about his rights, or Western tactics for deciding what is true. He knew a single vital word: 'refugee,' though even that was a hazy notion, a status that he didn't realise he'd have to claim, or fight for. He knew that the West had laws, humanitarian agreements, and money to care for vulnerable and endangered people. That seemed a simple enough thing: there was a pact between European countries to rescue those facing death, and that pact would save him. He packed some clothes and the passport in a rucksack, and headed to the airport. He had no money, no proof of his real identity.

For six hours over the Atlantic coastline, Solomon rubbed his thumb over the false passport in his pocket, his friend's face and name inside, his leg shaking as the hour drew closer. *My father vanished into a police station. My life was threatened. I need help.* None of the other passengers looked like refugees. They were European holidaymakers, or part of the Gambian diaspora. Would he be punished for entering the UK illegally? Surely no one expects paperwork with a machete hanging over your head. He would be okay, he reassured himself. He would get to safety, tell them what happened, then fill out whatever papers they needed.

In the immigration line at Manchester Airport, Solomon wondered when he should present himself. But as he was awaiting the officer's first question, his chance was snatched away: his passport had scanned as invalid – maybe his face didn't match the photo, or his friend, to protect himself, had reported it lost. The other passengers whispered as he was escorted away by immigration officers. Flanked by border police, he was whisked away to a dark corner of the airport, his heart in his mouth. The officers spoke fast English in strange accents. They asked dizzying questions one after another. He shrank back, allowing others to speak for him. The important thing right now, they seemed to say, was the false document he had carried. Maybe he would let them clear up that mess first, before asking for anything else.

And so, caught in the jaws of yet another police station, the very place he had lost his father, Solomon withdrew, never mentioning the assassination, the nights spent at the mercy of Guinean police. Adrift in the foreign noise, he forgot to tell them his story, or ask for help. He never requested asylum at the border.

★

Solomon spent that night in a small cell in the airport. He hardly slept. He thought of his wife and sons, his life back home. When would he see them again?

The next day in magistrates' court, his appointed lawyer made no arguments on his behalf. When Solomon was sentenced to twelve months for carrying a false document, the lawyer didn't seem surprised. With a plea entered and verdict handed down, his job was finished. Before he left, he told Solomon 'You can claim asylum after you get out. You'll need an immigration lawyer for that.'

What nobody told Solomon was that, if sentenced to twelve months or more in prison, an asylum seeker is automatically subject to deportation.

Solomon didn't see an immigration lawyer until he had finished his sentence.

For six months, he behaved as ordered and counted down the days to early release: to a long walk in a wooded place, to the summer sun on his shoulders, a private phone call with his sons. But on his last morning in prison, as he was preparing his bag, an officer told him that a fax had arrived from the immigration authorities. 'You're going to be held up for a while.' Instead of being released, Solomon was held for another week, then transferred to an immigration removals facility in Scotland, where he was served with a deportation order.

'For how long?' he asked.

Nobody could say. A detained person might be held for a week, a month, or years. There was no number to count down from, and so, in detention, Solomon began to count his days *up*.

His first asylum claim was refused. 'You should have claimed asylum at the border,' the first in a string of immigration lawyers said, 'that first day in the airport.' To win asylum now, after the deportation order had been issued, would be a near miracle.

'But I didn't know anything then!' said Solomon. 'I didn't even know the word *asylum*. They only wanted to talk about the passport.'

Two years after losing his father, Solomon disappeared into the mouth of a British detention centre.

Twice he was escorted by guards from the Home Office to the Guinean embassy, twice to the Gambian one, always with an order to request travel documents so that he could be deported. If he didn't cooperate in this, his own expulsion back into danger, he'd be marked down by his case officer. But by now, Solomon understood much more about the Home Office's immigration practices than he had in the airport. Each time a new lawyer arrived, he asked why he had to perform this charade. Each time, they shrugged and told him to obey. 'Sign this,' they said, taking great care with the forms that secured their legal aid money. So, Solomon went with the guards to the embassies. He sat silently in each interview, as the escorts waited in their car. Neither embassy could verify Solomon's identity, and so neither vouched for him. And with only someone else's European passport as ID, there was nowhere for Solomon to go but back to his cell.

He lost track of the number of times his asylum was rejected.

'We have to re-bill this,' the lawyers said as the closing gong to each refusal.

For years, Solomon lived in one detention centre after another, counting his days until they opened into a wasted chasm in his life, until the number grew so big, it surpassed one kola nut harvest, a school year, the time it takes for a child to walk, talk, ask questions. *This is worse than prison,* he thought. Maybe he didn't have to be complicit in this torture. He had refused to help with his own deportation, hadn't he? He had power. He had agency over his own body and mind. And so, one day, Solomon decided to do something other than counting.

*

On certain evenings, the smell of frying fish or chicken, peanut butter bubbling in stew, okra, and fluffy jollof rice filled the detention centre canteen. It made its way through the vents into the rooms where as many as twelve men slept on six bunk beds. It moved past the many locked doors that closed off the world. Guards wandered in, grabbed a plate, nodded to the African detainees who had once taken the time to explain each dish – the English, they all knew, are raised on the blandest foods. And so, it was a joy to offer them a taste of home, even if they're your warden. 'Solomon cooked tonight!' the guards would say. 'I know his food.' And everyone would briefly forget what had brought them together, in this canteen.

When chicken was frying, no one thought about the suicides. How one man tried to kill himself with strips from his bedsheets, another with the blade he had slipped into his mouth after shaving, how those who tried were punished in an isolation cell. When chicken was frying, Solomon could imagine his mother nearby, stirring the stews, unsticking the Benachin from the pot, seasoning the Domoda, telling him just how much peanut was enough.

Solomon worked as assistant chef from 9am to 5pm, earning one pound an hour. Sometimes detainees would come to him with a recipe, a request. His old favorites, or English staples like fish and chips. He noted the requests and cooked them when he had the right ingredients. Sometimes he talked to the chef about his life, but he had learned now not to trust anyone. Only to stay busy and conjure home with food.

In detention, his wife divorced him. 'I can't do this anymore,' she said on the phone. His boys grew up. Months later, Solomon had a call from his uncle. His mother had passed.

Now her dishes were his only way back to her.

Sometimes charity workers visited, gave the people in detention telephone cards, stayed to talk. He didn't trust most of them. He chatted politely. But then, Marian came back. As did Dermot, and he began writing to these new friends. He told them about his parents, the kola nut farm and his sons, who would be as tall as Solomon by now. One day, after three years in detention, he found the phone number for Detention Action in the library. The charity sent new lawyers, the kind who listened. One of them told him that he had been the victim of unlawful detention. Solomon had intuited this, but had stopped hoping someone else would see it, or that the bizarre laws would confirm it.

Now and then, his favourite immigration officer would come to Solomon with a pen and paper. 'Will you write down that recipe?' she'd say about that night's best dish, and Solomon wrote it down for her to try at home. She would return a few days later and tell him how well she had done. 'Solomon,' she said, 'I'm sorry your case is stuck.' If a newcomer to the detention centre became depressed, she sent them to Solomon's room. 'He will help you,' she said.

Every few weeks, a new arrival knocked on his door in panic, and asked variations of the same question. 'How are you still normal after all these years? Did you ever consider –'

'I can't do suicide,' he would say, 'This is life. There's always life.'

'Prison's better,' the newcomer would say, stumbling on the same image that strikes every refugee at one time or another.

'In prison, you can count your days down.'

'Life is a route,' Solomon often said. 'You have to work, go to the gym, cook something. They try to kill you with waiting. Try and relax. Don't put things too much in your head. Don't count the days up – that would be a mistake. Let's go watch Manchester United.'

One day, as he was cooking, an officer approached him. 'Solomon,' he said, 'We'll miss you and your food.'

'What do you mean?' he said, looking up from the half-chopped vegetables.

'You're going home today,' said the officer. 'I mean, you're getting out.'

It seemed that the new lawyer had argued his case and arranged his release.

Eight years after landing in Manchester, Solomon left yet another detention centre for what he hoped was the last time. His neighbours cried and wished him well.

That night, he slept in an unlocked building, in a room with only one other man. He was given his first weekly Tesco voucher for thirty-five pounds and reminded that he wasn't permitted to work.

A few years later, Solomon won his unlawful detention case. He spoke in front of the House of Commons about the mental torture of being made to wait, of becoming an object in a bureaucratic machine designed for the convenience of the Home Office.

★

Solomon has written home for his real papers. When he is granted the leave to remain, he will become a chef. He will cook West African food and fish and chips. Maybe he'll open a restaurant. Until then, he volunteers to speak to refugees whose spirits are broken, to help calm them, to remind them in their extreme isolation that life is waiting. Once, a long time ago, his father vanished into a police station. A few years later, Solomon too disappeared into one. He lost many years locked in that dark place, battling to get out. The worst crimes are committed under the cover of law. And yet, Solomon didn't succumb. He refused to wait, or to count his days. He lived. Each day he remembered his Baba's tired gait as he walked away. He cooked his mother's best dishes for his squandered neighbours, and he kept his eyes forward.

The Translator's Tale

as told by

Khodadad Mohammadi

Beginnings

MY NAME IS KHODADAD Mohammadi. I am from Afghanistan. From September 2017 to October 2020, I was in Greece.

You may have heard about Moria camp; the poor conditions, the long queues everywhere, the nervous people – but I had my own world there. I was working as a volunteer for different NGOs, helping the volunteers and refugees as a translator. Refugees in the camp didn't have access to any classes, or not enough, so I decided to teach English to anybody who wanted it; I had no classroom or equipment but the students were so kind to me and I tried to do the best I could.

For a while I taught English to two children; in doing this I felt a responsibility, and I tried to be back in my tent at the same time every evening to do the lesson. The camp was not safe, so I had to take them back to their tent after the lesson too. Before we started each lesson, they asked me to give them some candy in order for them to do their homework and learn well. They were funny and we grew close – of course, they were not as cheeky with my roommates! These experiences with my fellow camp-mates all made me forget what was going on in the camp, and in my life.

Forwards or backwards

Since leaving my home country, I have had to manage my life on my own and find my way. One way of coping has been to plan a step to take each year. In 2019, I decided my goal was to move further, and in October 2019 I left Moria Camp in Lesvos for Athens. I had already stayed on the island for two years, waiting so long in a place that has a dark history; I was afraid of staying any longer and losing any more time, so I decided to leave Greece, step by step.

In January 2020, after being in Athens for some time, I finally found a smuggler to help me leave Greece. It was not a good time for refugees, but of course this meant good business for smugglers. A rumour had spread everywhere that refugees were getting caught easily, and that there were fewer smugglers than before. Those smugglers were asking for large amounts of money (from four to seven thousand euros) and each was saying:

'I am the best; who can help you? Me!'

One was saying, 'I have a police partner at the airport and he will help you get on the plane without trouble...' but he was asking for seven thousand euros.

I decided to leave by ship and got a smuggler's phone number.

I talked to the smuggler on the telephone and convinced him that I was not a spy, and that I was simply a refugee going to find peace somewhere else. There is a third guy who works between the smuggler and the refugee, to open a bank account for both parties; when we arrive at our destination, the money is for the smuggler, not for the refugees. For example, I wanted to go to Italy, and they said when I arrive in Italy the money doesn't belong to me, but if I get caught it stays in the account and I have control over what to do with it. I received a code from the third person who kept the money, so without this code, nobody could have it, except me, unless I reached my destination. This whole process involves a lot of trust.

I left Athens for Patra; I had the address of where to go. When I arrived, another refugee came to take me to a house. When we were close to the address, he looked around to see if the police were following me and told me where to go to make sure we were safe. We were hiding in a broken house; it seemed the house had been empty for a long time. During the day, no one moved, but at night a lot of activities happened.

On the second night, someone called out –

'Who is ready for an orange game?'

An 'orange game' is an illegal movement; for example, crossing a border, taking two portions of food at dinner, maybe stealing. I learned this along the way and heard it in Moria camp a lot. Amongst refugees, it is a common phrase, they all know what it means.

So I thought: it would be funny if we left Greece for Italy in a truck that carries oranges! I had heard it before – that people use any kind of vehicle to travel to Italy.

On the third night, the smuggler called out –

'Be ready! Tonight, we have a game – a real game! To send you to Italy!'

There were five smugglers, who had found an orange truck going to Italy.

The truck was parked close to a farm, where nobody was there to see us.

We took out around 40 boxes of oranges and threw them away. We made a small space to sit – one metre wide and two metres long with a height of 70 centimetres for ten people. We could have a bottle of water, some food, a bottle to pee in; it would take three days to arrive in Italy.

We stayed for three or four hours in the truck, quietly waiting. The driver came and the truck started moving; everyone was stressed, excited, worried, and happy. We were talking very slowly and carefully, people were wishing and hoping to reach Italy. Someone was saying, 'please don't talk and put your phones on silent,' someone else, 'please help each other to sit comfortably,' and some joking, 'please don't fart we need to be conscious!' I was just hoping; whatever happened was out of our control now.

We were driving for hours but we never arrived at the ship.

We grew worried, and after maybe four hours we said, 'no, it is not going to Italy'. Someone said, 'maybe it will go to Tirana and then Italy', but we couldn't risk going to Turkey.

We started knocking and shouting to stop the truck. The driver stopped and opened the door, noticed that we were refugees, closed it immediately and called the police.

When we saw the police, we said 'it's over; the police will send us to Athens anyway,' but I didn't expect to be detained for a long time. I said to myself 'shit', but I was talking to the police, trying to act like nothing had happened.

In the end, we stayed in the police station for one night in two groups. Six people were released, and the rest transferred to a detention centre somewhere else. Four of us stayed for three weeks waiting for a bus to move us to Athens.

In police custody, we had lots of fun; we made playing cards out of paper, a ball with disposable food dishes... When the day came to leave for Athens, we were moved to a closed camp by the name of Mondalisia. Mondalisia is a very big closed camp with high security that houses refugees with permit issues, including families, singles, minors and even sick people.

But after about three weeks, they sent me back to Lesvos with other people like me, and we were moved to Moria detention centre.

Life in A1

In Moria detention centre, there are two sections with about two hundred refugees. It is a heavily secured area surrounded by barbed wire that includes twelve containers. I was staying in room A1. In A1 there were fifteen people, all from different countries: Afghanistan, and Arab and African countries.

Most of us had been there more than six months, so we knew each other very well.

Life in detention is the second university. You can learn a lot in detention that it isn't possible to learn anywhere else. It depends on who you are and how you look at yourself and the whole situation, and the other refugees that you are together with.

Not only can you learn a new language, painting or even tattooing, but you also learn a new way of behaving and being patient. All this makes people smarter than before. When people suffer from being imprisoned and they have made a mistake or committed a crime, then this is the place where they can rethink and find out what they should or can do in the future.

I saw it for myself in a junkie friend who suffered a lot, so it was a good time for him to stabilise himself and build his life again. With the help of others, he was able to quit heroin. The first day, he was ill and kept saying 'just give me a massage and sleeping pills.' We served and helped him for a few days until he got better. Mentally, we were trying to keep him relaxed and didn't let him talk to the guy who was bringing heroin to him and other junkies in detention, and finally, we were successful without a doctor or medicine.

What you are reading right now is what I started to write in detention.

Everyone knows that people in the centre have problems. This is normal – in prison people don't behave like people outside. This is especially true if someone has mental health issues. It is difficult to bear in the centre, and most of the people there had some kind of mental health issues. It was always very loud and noisy. Some listened to loud music and people yelled at each other often.

Mamo prayed loudly several times a day – he was arguing with his God, complaining about what hadn't happened in his life, or something bad that had. He used different languages while praying. We asked him to pray quietly, but he said: 'No, it's better loud.'

And we said: 'Oh, yes, because God will hear you better!'

He was talking to himself repeatedly, speaking to all the people who had hurt him in his life and he cursed them, wished bad things would happen to them.

It was boring to hear all these stories, for we had heard them a hundred times already. Sometimes, when he would get really loud and not want to stop, we would approach him and say: 'We will hit you if you don't stop now!' Mostly it worked and he shut up.

But overall, we tried to keep calm and be friendly. We were the Afghan team; we were five guys, and we were like a family. We did our best to help each other. I did the writing: I wrote letters to the asylum services and to lawyers, asking for help and explaining cases. It was good to do something. We washed each other's clothes, we played games, we made jokes, danced and talked. We shared our experiences about how we came to be there. We tried to keep the negative thoughts away, encourage each other and talk about the good days we'd had in the past.

Whatever we possessed, we shared it with everyone in our group.

Once a week, a market guy came, and we bought vegetables and spices to improve the daily food and pack baskets for everybody. We put the money together, everybody gave as much as they could afford.

We said to the people without money: 'Brother, don't feel strange, take it.'

Sometimes we shared one cigarette between five people. For fun, we would mark little signs for how much everybody could smoke, so each had the same.

I remember how it was at the beginning: I felt very strange, frustrated and lost.

But it changed. We changed; we made our own world inside A1. My name in there was 'Tarjoman', this means translator. Many of my friends didn't speak good English, so I translated for them. I also speak a little Greek and so I could communicate with the policemen who didn't speak English.

I translated, I had a good job in there, and sometimes I did English lessons for the others. Everyone offered their skills to each other; it was a good way of being creative and changing our situation into something better.

We were aware of what was going on outside; we heard about coronavirus, which was changing the whole world. During lockdown, we were sorry for the big change outside, but we said: 'So now everyone in the whole world is in prison, it's just that our prison is a bit smaller!'

Yes, we spent our time like this, and talked through the window with people outside. Once, we told some guys: 'Hey, do you know, there is a ship picking up refugees, it can swim and it can fly. It will come to Moria Street very soon and it will bring you to England, Germany or wherever you want to go!'

They asked: 'Really? Is that true?' and laughed a lot.

Once, we said to someone, who told us how good it feels to be free, that the sea will come and rise up and everything and every person will be floating soon. He said, full of worries: 'Oh my god...'

Sometimes we had fun with the police, too. When the electricity ran out, we started a big show in the darkness. People imitated different animal sounds like maaaaaaa, wawawawa, meyou meyou meyou, qoud qoudagh.

And the police shouted: 'It is not a zoo here! Shut up!'

In the summertime it was terribly hot outside. Twice a day we were let out of our room for 30 minutes in the courtyard. Each time, we had a water fight and wet each other to get cool and danced in front of the police. They laughed and it made them happy as well.

That's the way our life was.

We have the right to be free, to have a normal life, to be happy. If they take this life from us, we have to care for it ourselves, no matter where we are.

Strange world

It's been one week that I have been free now. Two days after I left, they locked down the whole camp because of coronavirus. Of course, I didn't know that. But, wow, I'm really a lucky man!

It was Friday night, at around 11pm. We all had our phones and were busy. I was watching a movie on my bed. A police officer called my name three times.

I responded, 'Yes, I'm here.'

He said, 'Prepare yourself, you are free!'

I said, 'No way – really?'

Police said, 'Yes, Malaka, take your stuff and leave.' I was very, very happy! My friends were happy and sad. Everyone hugged me and wished me well. They said, 'Don't forget us! Come to see us and go on helping us.'

I said, 'Don't worry! I won't forget you, but you will be free very soon, too! I'll try my best!'

★

I went to visit a friend in Moria camp. I had a look at my old tent, where I stayed for two years. I used to call it The White House. My friend's tent is nearby. He's running a small business in his room, selling cigarettes and different kinds of drinks. After a few minutes of talking, I took a deep breath.

My friend said: 'Are you hungry?'

I said, 'No, no.' I wasn't hungry although I hadn't eaten for a long time.

He smiled and said, 'I know how you feel', and he opened a cold Coca-Cola. That was the best moment! It was perfect. It was a moment you normally see in movies, but now I experienced it. While drinking the Coca-Cola I thought to myself: *I'm free now!* I was very excited.

I texted a message to a good friend. We have known each other for three years and she had been helping me a lot. She couldn't believe it. I sent a picture to prove it. So, she came in her car to take me to her house in Mytiline.

I slept very well that night, although it was much hotter than in our container. And it was noisy, too. But I enjoyed it because I was finally free and sure about the next step.

The next day we had a beautiful breakfast and then everyone planned what they would do. My plan was clear: I had to go swimming! I went swimming with a friend and there she took a picture of me and I sent it to all my friends. I had a really nice time at this place. My friend introduced me to the new lockdown rules: she gave me a mask and said, 'The most necessary thing you need in these times!'

And I was trying to learn how everything has changed.

Still, I feel very strange in this time that has changed the world. It's horrible, this sickness is really harming people, everything has stopped: communication, learning, meeting, official works, freedom. Especially for refugees, now it's very difficult. Since being released, I have tried to have some fun and enjoy my freedom, but I still have problems to solve!

Now I am outside, but my mind is still in detention. My phone is with me all the time. I can use it as long as I want to without hiding it. Inside, I was using a phone which was smuggled in. It was important that nobody should catch me. If the police were to discover it, they would take it away until the end of our detention, and assign some other kind of punishment, too.

If the police found anything that was not allowed, they took it away. We had to ask for nail clippers from the police, but they didn't give them to us. I was cutting my nails with a sharpener or a razor. Even the sharpener was illegal. So outside, I started doing the same. My friend watched me and laughed.

He shook his head, saying, 'No, no it can't be good, what you are doing. You really have got some strange new habits. But now you are not detained anymore so try to forget what you are dealing with. Take my clippers.' When I sleep now, I still feel that I have to use earplugs even if it is not noisy because I am used to wearing them every night.

Now I am staying with a friend, resting my soul and waiting for the next step, which I believe will be one of the best steps. Since being released, I have been focusing on the next plan. I have been waiting for three years in Greece; it's been good but not enough, I need asylum and access to my future. This could be my last chance to get out of Greece before they deport me. I want to leave Greece as soon as possible.

The Future

Today, 19th January 2021, I looked at the pictures of three years ago in Greece, the pictures that reminded me of how it was. For a short time, I lived once again in those moments. I could feel what happened. I felt cold, hot, hungry, tired, happy... I was back there in that long food line again. Now these are only memories, and I am glad to have met great people in those times.

Since November 2020 I have been in Germany. It marks the end of part of my life and the beginning of another, one with a big difference and higher quality! Here, refugees can go to school, they have their own apartments, health care and lots of other support. I am very happy to be here and feel relaxed in my chest. No more lines, no more Moria, no more watching grumpy faces!

It seems I crossed many borders and circumstances; hardship and good times, too, to get here.

The Running Person's Tale

as told to

Philippe Sands

'I DESERVE TO BE a migrant. I don't want money. I don't want things to be given to me. I'm not useless. I can be useful for someone.'

Al Beider, as I shall call him, is in his twenties and living in a hotel on the Wembley Way, near the famous football stadium, which serves today as a detention centre. Born in the town of Al Bayda, near the centre of Yemen, he arrived in Britain a little over a year ago, hoping to make a new life, to become a medical doctor. This is a path he has pursued since childhood, following the death of his father when he was just six years old.

Al is an asylum seeker. He is fearful of being returned to the country of his birth, which is today the site of a proxy war between Iran and Saudi Arabia, one that is being fought with weaponry supplied by the government of the country of his current residence.

He tells me the year he was born with a warm and intelligent smile. He does not offer the appearance of a man diminished by his recent experiences. Yemen was a united country back then, and his mother and father joined from different parts. 'I belong to the United Yemen, and I believe in that in a political sense, but I have two bloods.' He is proud of the town of his birth, a place renowned for its fighters and tribes.

'My mother belongs to the city where I was born, she belongs to the north. My dad belonged to the west. After the British Empire left, his father had problems with the government, so he ran away to Al Bayda. That was where my parents met. They had a traditional marriage, one in the normal Islamic way. It wasn't love, or something like that which brought them together. It was a traditional set up.'

The couple raised three boys, Al is the youngest. The family moved to Jeddah, in Saudi Arabia, he says, because of 'the poor life' in Yemen, without electricity or water. 'An amazing city,' he says, a place where he never felt himself to be a stranger, at least not until he reached the age of eighteen. 'As a child, I had the same accent as everyone else, no one could recognise that I was a foreigner.'

His father died when he was seven, during his third year at school. 'I didn't know much about him,' Al says, 'I loved him, he loved me.' He pauses. 'I think if he had lived I would not be here today, calling you from a room in Wembley. I would not be the person I am.'

After his father's death, the family remained in Saudi Arabia. His mother is still there, with the two other sons about whom Al is somewhat reticent to speak. His difficulties began after he left school. 'I had a dream, because my dad died from Hepatitis C, I wanted to be a doctor.' Al too had been ill, spending three months in hospital, also with hepatitis. As a foreigner he was unable to gain entrance to a university in Saudi Arabia, so he decided to return to Yemen.

Back in Sana'a, he is in for a shock. His school certificate is Saudi, which means he can't get a scholarship or access to a public university in Yemen. 'No, I said to myself, I will study to be a doctor, whatever it costs me. I am stubborn.'

He gets a place at a Science and Technology University, a private institution. For a year he studies medicine. It is tough, because of the money, because he is far away from his mother and older brothers, those who guide him, and because war has come to the country.

'The war got worse while I was there. Houthi rebels were fighting against the government, and in 2014 they started to become stronger, supported by Iran, against a government supported by the Saudis.' He is questioned by Houthi rebels, about his strange ID card and accent, which are different from other people. 'Because I grew up in Saudi Arabia, they felt like I didn't belong to the place. Anyone who speaks with me in my mother language, Arabic, will think I am Saudi.'

The difficulties mount. Why doesn't he have internal ID? Is he proud of Yemen? Does he have a property in Sana'a? 'I said yes, I have a house. They took me to my house; they sat with me for three days, when they learned I came from Saudi Arabia, from Jeddah, they think that I can be helpful for them. They were rough with me. They screamed. They beat me. Then someone came who said they knew my family and all my tribe.'

As soon as he can, he leaves Yemen to return to Saudi Arabia. He is unable to find work, and unwilling to take a job that would require him to hand over his passport. 'I don't want anyone to own me, to hold my passport so I can't leave. I don't want to be a modern slave.'

He enrols at another university, this time in business studies. 'Little by little, I grew up, I started to be mature, I learned what is happening. I understand I will not belong to Saudi Arabia, I am a foreigner.'

On the side, to earn money to pay for university, he works for a local transportation and taxi company. 'A bit like Uber,' he explains. He is an Assistant Project Manager, one who dresses and sounds like a Saudi although, as he is at pains to point out, the company knows he is not a Saudi.

The outsider continues along this path for five more years. 'I had a good life and a bad life.' A good life because it is stable and he has a plan, to graduate from the university. A bad life because after graduation he knows he will not be able to work freely in Saudi Arabia: 'Because I am not from here, so I will not be able to have what I want or what I can achieve in my life.'

In 2016 he travels to Malaysia, to perfect his English. 'I met a girl from Spain, a Muslim, another tourist, and little by little we fell in love.' When he returns to Saudi Arabia, they stay in touch, and he comes to realise that he is 'living in the shadows,' unlike people in Europe and North America, those 'who can aspire to, imagine, another life, those who can choose what they want and then do it, who have a freedom.'

He and the girl meet again, in Egypt and in Jordan. He is unable to obtain a visa to travel to visit her in Spain. 'So we broke up, in 2018, because I could not go to her country.'

After the break-up, he returns to Yemen, to test the life there. He studies for another year, and comes to understand the people there have a different mentality. 'I came to the conclusion that I had to leave. But to where? Someone said, "Go to Mauritania."' Mauritania, he was told, would allow him to get to Morocco, and then to the nearest European country, Spain. 'I speak English, I love a girl, I speak a little Spanish, so why not? I can do great things. I can support a government. I can be political, I can be ideological. I can even be gay if I want! It's not like Saudi Arabia, where you have to conform. I am not that person.'

And so he goes, to Mauritania. It takes him three days. And from there he goes to the desert of Mali, where he pays to be driven to a city. Then on to Algeria, for fifteen days, a place of smugglers looking to make a quick buck. Then to Morocco, for a month, looking for a route to Spain. 'And then, finally,' he says, 'I got my legs in a Spanish place, where the soldiers meet me. They were a little bit nice, until the second day.'

He is returned to a camp in Melila, a Spanish enclave that shares a border with Morocco. He claims asylum, seeking humanitarian protection from the civil war in Yemen. 'My country,' he calls it, although he hardly loves it. Three months later he is sent to a different camp, this time on the Spanish mainland – 'lots of problems there, lots of thieves' – and then he is cast out onto the street, left to rely on charities to provide food and accommodation.

He gets himself to Barcelona, to meet up with his former girlfriend, but it doesn't work out, not 'as I wished'. His asylum application will be processed, but only after a year. In the meantime, he has a right to stay. 'Should I stay for one year,' he asks, 'living on the street?'

Spain is tough, so is living on the street. So he decides to try his luck in France. By now he has no money and has lost his passport, in Algeria. Without it, friends will find it hard to send him money. In Paris he befriends some Roma, who speak a little Spanish, so they understand that he is homeless. They take him under their wing. 'I went with them, stealing to survive.'

Life is hard. Everywhere he goes life seems to be hard. Someone says, 'Go to the Britain!' 'Why?' he asks. 'Because you speak the language.' He decides to try, without money. On 1 January he swims from a beach near Calais, hoping to get past the security fences around the port and onto a ferry. It is cold, there's a swell in the sea, he fails. 'I was going to the deep, I thought the end of my life was coming. I was screaming, but no one is there, because they are celebrating in the first hour of new year. No one hears me.'

He saves himself and looks for another way. This time he and someone else he has met will pay a smuggler. 'We entered the UK, I applied for my asylum immediately. They asked a few questions. How old are you? I have a baby face, people told me to say I was sixteen. I told them the truth. Now I realise I should have lied.'

He is detained at an Immigration Removal Centre, near an airport. He meets criminals awaiting deportation. 'In the end, I stay with them, they were nice, gave me money because the food in the detention centre was not good, and cigarettes. Here, I started to smoke!'

The pandemic erupts in the spring of 2020. After a month he is released, sent to a hostel. He is told he must share a bed. 'With someone I don't know, during the pandemic!' He calls an advice line, they tell him to call the police. 'I just came from detention but I want to go back, please return me to detention – I cannot share a bed with someone else.'

He is sent to Cardiff. Three weeks there.

He is sent to Swansea. Two months there.

He is sent to Luton. Another two months.

Al Beider is a long way from Al Bayda.

He receives a letter telling him to go to Croydon, to Lunar House, to sign a document.

He goes. Then he is sent to a new home, the place from where he speaks, a hotel that doubles up as a detention centre. On the Wembley Way, in the shadow of the famous stadium.

And the future?

'I cannot go back to Yemen. The Houthi rebels would try to recruit me again, make me take a job, give me a gun and tell me to go and fight.'

He is articulate.

'I am running from death, I am running for my dreams.'

He still has a family.

'I am in contact with my mother, we are close.'

He has hopes.

'I want an identity. I don't want anything from this government. I don't want a holiday in a hotel. I want to stay to have a life. I want opportunity. I want freedom.'

He is very human.

'I don't want to belong to anyone. From the time I was born until now, I have never felt like I belonged, not to a country or a community. I have never had a say in any decision about things going on around me.'

He can still smile.

'Why did I come here? Because they say this is a place with humanity.'

The Daughter's Tale

as told by

Natalia Sierra

Natalia

I DECIDED TO JOIN film school without much idea of what being a filmmaker entailed. The notion of making movies and travelling the world, attending film festivals and watching more movies, was enough for me to sign up for a five-year university course. To my surprise, and very early on, I discovered how rich, profound, versatile, challenging and adventurous making movies was. We learned about film history and anthropology; scriptwriting and Greek literature; art direction, colour theory, design; acting and directing; casting actors, finding locations; filming, editing, working with musicians; then finally, the marketing ordeal that the distribution of a film requires. It was paradise for me. It was a space for imagination, creation, fiction and reality. I loved engaging with the acting crew, the creatives, the location owners, the audience in the cinema. Making documentaries became my career. It was the perfect excuse for me to jump into strangers' lives and learn about their way of being, thinking, working. The camera became an ideal companion. When I look back, I see how empowered I was by the dynamic of observing without being observed; a story that was not mine; experiencing realities that I could exit at any time.

I had one semester left to do in order to graduate from university, when my family and I decided to flee Colombia and look for political asylum in Switzerland. We were being persecuted and leaving was our last resort. Arriving in Switzerland, it was as if we had slipped into a nightmare from which it was not possible to wake. I felt so far away from the person I used to be. We lived in refugee centres in dehumanising conditions. We experienced the absence of privacy, silence and autonomy. We had to redefine our ideas of identity. Our passports, driver's licenses, and identity cards were confiscated. We had to face our darkest demons to find hope. We had to fight for our right to security, our right to be recognised as refugees, by exposing our most intimate and painful memories to immigration officers who didn't trust what we told them to prove that our lives were truly endangered.

As we have endured this journey, I have been looking back to find traces of why I decided to write about my experience as a refugee. I remember how, in the first years, my mother urged me to make a documentary about our lives as asylum seekers. She would say something like *We might never live in a refugee centre again, you must film this. The world needs to know about this awful place.* But I couldn't pick up my cell phone and record a single second of my life. Back in Colombia, I was behind the camera, and that felt safe. Here in Switzerland, I was not willing to place myself in front of the camera to be seen, judged and pointed at.

That is how writing found me. Every experience of this journey as a refugee is like a flame inside of me, desperate to escape before it burns me a little bit more inside. These stories were born from the step of courage my mother, brother and sister-in-law took by remembering and sharing their memories with me.

Laura
27 June, 2016
Choachi, Colombia

I was 19 years old when Gabriel and I got married. Our wedding took place at a beautiful villa in a small town surrounded by green mountains and palm trees. My family drove for hours to get there; our friends left the big city to join us. We felt blessed and happy. Being a grown-up was fun at that time.

And yet, despite the festive atmosphere, the continuous toasts by my uncles, the children's laughter, the music, the spontaneous dancing, the surreal sunset and our overwhelming love for each other, no one could hide the sadness that farewells carry. I knew the tears in my parent's eyes were not only of joy.

Not long before our wedding, Gabriel told me about the threats his family was receiving because of the human rights legal work his mother was performing. One month after our wedding, we fled Colombia and came to Switzerland. We joked about having a fancy honeymoon in the Swiss Alps. Our wedding was not only a celebration of love and commitment, but also a parting. It was one of the last moments I felt at home.

★

5 August, 2016,
Kreuzlingen, Switzerland

I was jet-lagged, tired and confused. The sun was hitting our faces as we walked from the train station carrying our heavy suitcases. I was quiet and absent. I could tell Gabriel also wanted to keep the silence, but forced himself to take part in the conversations his mother and sister were having. They sounded somehow cheerful. As we walked, a big grey and hostile building stood in front of us. The building was an absurd and scary element in the middle of picturesque old houses. The surroundings were quiet and the town felt lonely.

We walked to the glass shelter by the entrance. Gabriel's mother was fierce when talking to the security guards on the other side of the glass. They didn't seem surprised about our request to claim asylum in this building. As they let us in, a cold and frightening feeling travelled through my body. I tried reaching for Gabriel's hand, but he was far away in the next hallway. The place seemed like a prison you would see in a TV series: long hallways, on the one side a big room with long tables and chairs; on the other, an indoor patio with tall grey walls and what looked like a tiny metal playground from a Nazi movie. The place was terrible and I felt as if my eyes were detached from my body, and whatever I was seeing wasn't really there, wasn't true.

We were conducted to a glass room facing the patio. There was a shelter and they asked us to fill out a long questionnaire. Six other people were waiting in this room with us. They looked scared, tired, hungry and mostly helpless. Their kids were crying and the parents were trying to figure out what to write in the questionnaire. Bulky security guards watched us constantly and as the family asked about what to put in the questionnaire, they got aggressive and spoke to them as if they were prisoners. I could only hear the family saying "Kurdistan". A country I had never heard of before.

Some hours later, a nice young man came to us and introduced himself as part of the staff. He was the first friendly face I had seen since our arrival. Despite his attempts to make us feel less awkward, I know we all felt disgusted, disoriented and homesick. His name was Mateo and he would take us to our sleeping quarters.

The big room with tables was the eating area. There were around 30 people sitting at the tables. I looked at the patio and saw some kids running around. Everyone sat or stood against the glass windows or the tall walls. I saw many men smoking.

It was the first time in my life I saw women wearing head scarves. Everyone turned to look at us, as if we were a magnet. The men had intense and angry eyes, and I felt them through my body.

The hallway felt endless. Then there were many stairways. The floors were white and the place was cold. Many people from all kinds of nationalities walked up and down the stairs, as if they were teenagers running around school hallways in the break. All of them stared at us, some said something; some winked their eyes, some laughed. I couldn't understand a word. I couldn't process a thought. I couldn't let go of Gabriel's hand.

As Mateo took us to the basement, for a second I came back to myself and became aware of my breath. I smelt sweat and urine, the odours were so strong I felt like vomiting and remembered I hadn't had any food in hours. The basement area felt like a camp. There was a huge metal door that Mateo asked Claudia to open *for the girls to enter.* There were the showers: an open beige room, without any divisions, just water pouring out of the walls. Some elder women were showering naked and I felt like an intruder.

As we moved on, I tried to look at Gabriel's face. His green eyes were grey and his skin was paler than ever. He tried smiling, but his mouth looked stiff and dry. He squeezed my hand. We walked upstairs. Each floor had many doors, all were closed.

Our dormitory was on the top floor. Mateo showed us the bathrooms. This time I rushed to open the door; I felt like vomiting again. I forced myself not to breathe. There was no toilet, but a metallic floor with water running. I rushed to open the next door and it looked the same. I vomited and it felt as if my soul was being poured onto that shiny floor. The toilet paper was on the floor and it was wet.

I came out of the booth and saw Natalia's face in the tiny mirror hanging on the wall. She looked haggard, as if she had aged ten years in the past few hours. She put water on her face and washed her hands intensively. I thought she was wishing to wash this feeling off herself. Our eyes crossed in the mirror. We saw that we were as vulnerable as we had ever been.

We left the toilet area and were taken to the dormitories. I felt desperate to be in my bed, at home, to feel both the warmth and coolness one feels when getting under the sheets after a long, cold day. The room had bunkbeds and a big window facing the patio; you could also see the sky and some railway bridges. In front of the beds, there were lockers, just like the ones you find in a gym or in a high school. Women from every continent occupied the beds.

I kept on holding Gabriel's hand until I heard Mateo's voice clearly for the first time: *These are the dormitories for women and kids; the men sleep on the other side of the building.* Gabriel looked around, as if looking for someone to confirm what we had just heard. We hugged strongly, kissed softly and he whispered in my ear *Te veo pronto, mi amor.*

Claudia

I wandered around our apartment. It was almost empty, but there were still some plants a friend had to pick up and some piles of documents I needed to revise. The velvet armchair was in its usual spot facing the window. The departure date was close, nonetheless, I couldn't imagine the idea of giving away the last piece of furniture I had from my mother. I always remember how much she adored that piece. My own home felt familiar and alien at the same time. Boxes, suitcases, photo albums and clothes were lying all over the living room.

It was silent and the night was dark. Gabriel was not home that night and Natalia was sleeping in her room. Whenever one of my children was not at home, I would have trouble sleeping, worrying something bad would happen to them. As they grew up, it became natural not to sleep through the night until I heard the door opening or the phone ringing. Even though they were in their twenties and Gabriel had just got married, I cared for them as much as I did when they were little.

No one had forced me to advocate for people's rights. I owned every decision I made and if I had to, I would do it again. But the past few months had been exhausting. Looking through the window I spotted tiny city lights in the distance. I felt an urgency to disappear, to be someone else. I prayed. *I can only do this with your guidance. I can only do this with your strength. I can only do this by faith.*

I heard a firm and loving voice. *I am with you. My plans are greater than yours. I am sending you and your loved ones to bring light and justice. Do not be afraid.*

★

5 August, 2016
Kreuzlingen, Switzerland

I knew there were going to be many procedures, paperwork, interviews and hard times. Even so, I could never imagine what it is to be stripped of your essential belonging, stripped of your identity.

The room was tiny, with grey walls and white lamps on the ceiling. There was a long metallic table. The security guard was a tough lady in her late twenties. I saw her commanding some other security guards before we entered this room. I also saw how, deep inside herself, she felt ashamed for what she was about to do.

She placed my suitcase on the table. I stood back and leaned against the wall. I wished for a chair to sit on, because my legs shook. She put on some plastic gloves and, without any delicacy, took everything out of my suitcase and inspected blouse after blouse, undergarment after undergarment, book after book, page after page. She checked the pockets of my pants, the compartments of my wallet, the liquids in my cosmetics.

She emptied my wallet in front of my eyes; took my driver's license, identification card, passport, credit cards, USB stick, nail clippers, earrings and other small objects. I thought of the many years I had been carrying those same documents with me, most of them for over 35 years. Now, this complete stranger on the other side of the world was carefully selecting and deciding which ones I no longer needed. For a second I thought about ripping my passport out of her hands and holding it tightly to my chest. The idea felt so childish I laughed at myself. She turned to me and said *Is there something funny Ms Poveda?*

I had written a document explaining how my position as a lawyer had forced us to flee Colombia two days before and seek political asylum in Switzerland. The letter, two suitcases with documents proving my legal work in Colombia, and the documentary Natalia and Gabriel had made, was all we had to request asylum. We knew nobody in Switzerland, we had made no contact with the embassy nor with any NGO. I wouldn't take that risk. Our closest friends and family thought we were coming for a few months until things would hopefully settle down in Colombia. They made this assumption because I never shared how serious the threats were. The past three years of our lives had been anything but normal: moving home every four months, changing telephone numbers constantly, going to the US for weeks, sometimes just weekends in order to confuse our persecutors. We had become like nomads and adapted quickly to the new reality, but the three of us knew it couldn't last for too long. But then, that terrible incident with Laura and the two persecutors that threatened her. That was the trigger for our decision to flee.

An hour passed and I sat on the floor, defenceless. The woman asked me to stand up and checked my whole body with her sticky white gloves. I saw all my belongings on that cold table, as if they were of no use; banal things, leftovers of a past, precious life.

Natalia
16 March, 2021
Zurich, Switzerland

It has become complex to remember my life in Colombia. It has been almost five years since we left. I feel as if I have lived two completely different lives in two different universes. People often ask me if I miss home; every time, I need to pause and ask myself that question before responding with something generic or automatic. Do I miss home?

I never felt fully comfortable in Bogota. I grew up with a strong awareness of the danger surrounding me. Any stranger in the street could feel like a possible robber, killer or rapist to me. Whenever I walked alone in the streets, I would get close to a group of strangers and act as if I was with them. I always hid important objects in random and secret places around the house, in case someone broke in to take our valuables. Every time I got on a bus I would sit right next to the driver to feel safer. It always intrigued me how everyone else seemed to cope with life so unguarded, and rarely got robbed or hurt. But even with my paranoia, I was a fearless person in regard to my dreams and aspirations. I was hopeful and hyperactive and had beautiful adventures I treasured in my life.

What I miss about home is the feeling of possibilities. I miss knowing how things work and moving around them. I miss how I would know exactly what to say to a security guard in a museum when it was about to close, so that he or she would let me in anyway. I miss visiting small towns and chatting with owners of tiny shops about trivial things. I miss driving to my father's house in the mountains without announcement and being welcomed as if he was waiting for me. I miss sitting in my grandmother's rocking chair on the balcony and hearing about her anecdotes as a young au pair in Belgium. I miss the feeling of belonging and fellowship. I miss the feeling of home.

★

12 August, 2016
Kreuzlingen, Switzerland

We spread our towels out on the grass. My mother lay with modesty while I took off my summer dress, watching the sun shine over the diamond-like water of the lake. I closed my eyes for a few minutes and only thought about the mighty and turquoise ocean in Colombia.

My mother and I have been very close. We always shared like friends. Many times we lay next to each other, respecting the silence and nourishing the present moment. Before she asked me to, I knew when she wanted to have some sunscreen and cold water on her back. It was a natural dynamic for both of us when we were sunbathing. On that short summer afternoon, I was able to transport myself to a contented, peaceful and familiar life.

Suddenly and eagerly my mother got up and said, *Naty, it's already 4pm*. I saw my mother acting without thinking too much; she was resigned and determined not to give me the space to complain or question, a quality of hers that always made me crazy. The following minutes were accelerated. We packed our few things and moved away from the lake. A few metres ahead, we joined the groups of people walking towards our destination, like every afternoon.

We were already approaching the refugee centre, when I noticed my brother and his wife Laura were not around. Before going back, we would usually meet by the entrance. The despair gradually grew in me as I looked for them in the crowd. My mom seemed worried and weary. We were the last in line, and the security guards gestured us inside and pointed at the watches on their wrists. They were not there. Maybe they are already in, I thought to myself.

Inside, the heat and the smell of sweat was fatal. Although we had arrived a week ago, I could not get used to such a strong smell. I went to the patio hoping to see them. Then to the communal dining room, where some children played with old wooden toys and German board games. I ran upstairs to the room we shared with twelve other women. Later, to the men's room. The storm in my head grew potently and brought thoughts of confusion, anger and frustration.

I ran to look for my mother and when she saw my anxiety, she tried to calm me down. *I talked to the guards and it is allowed to sleep outside from Friday night to Sunday night. Surely they have just lost track of time and will sleep in a park, I guess.* I looked around and felt a deep hatred for that place, for the glass doors and the security guards who stood by them all day and night. I tried to find a glimpse of peace in my mother's eyes, but her look of resignation gave me chills. I couldn't breathe. I needed to get out of that place. I needed to run freely. I needed to jump into the lake and swim to the bottom. I needed to fly and escape, just like they did.

I ran to the patio and felt everyone's gaze on me. I looked for the loneliest corner there was. I tried to take a deep breath but the air felt disgusting to me. Defeated, I threw myself to the ground and the storm began to come out of my eyes.

Children were playing in the small playground and immediately approached me, as they usually did, so that we could play hide and seek or read a book together. Their tenderness and naivety made me feel worse. Their mothers came to give me tissues and water to drink. Their gestures were compassionate and kind. The men and youngsters sat next to me to ask if I was okay, if I wanted a cigarette or if they should call my mother. At the bottom of my being, I felt a sense of solidarity and union I have never experienced before or again since.

An older man whom I feared and respected, and with whom I had never spoken, approached me. He knelt, looked at me with his marine green and sad eyes, and said in his broken English, *If you cry, we cry.*

I longed to be alone like never before. The showers were my last hope. It was empty and I sat on a long bench where we put our towels before bathing. My mouth was completely dry and I had a boundless thirst, but didn't have the strength to get up. Never in my life have I felt like a prisoner until that day. It was absurd not to be able to be outside with my brother and Laura. It was overwhelming to think about the five hours I had before it was dark, before I could close my eyes and sleep.

My mother entered the showers with a couple of our roommates, young and cheerful ladies with whom I always chatted and shared pastries in the evenings. They were terrified to see me like that. I thought I heard my mother's heart break like a glass vessel.

The Chef's Tale

as told to

Simon Smith

WE MEET ONLINE NOT by Skype but via Zoom, it could have been Skype, but no it's Zoom we use, in this new locked down reality, a new kind of imprisonment we all now share, in slow-mo, distanced, time-stopped. Out of the pixelated shadowlands your face appears, glasses reflecting back at the screen its blue light, thick beard, a smile. The background is a bland off-white wall, a curtain half-drawn behind you, and half-opened. You could be anywhere. Or nowhere. Or seemingly locked into a non-place, floating on the ether of cyberspace. Suspended animation.

You start to speak, a voice full of surprises, out of the Midlands, a timbre and tone already naturalised, already arrived, roots down, with only the odd skip back to its original lilt, like a faint trace, a ghost. You introduce yourself as S. You speak, the history and the story pours out – amnesties, coups, presidents imprisoned, civil unrest, corrupt governments, revolts, phones being tapped – the ebb and flow of hope and then despair. A nation reinvented, and its story retold to suit each incoming faction in charge, discrediting the last. History and stories retold, a nation reinvented. Tides in, then tides out. The ever-present army, with the recurrent pretext and excuse of 'corruption,' an excuse for action, repression, terror. Your family is involved in local politics. S, you are a student leader, you are taken into custody for no reason on trumped-up charges of attempted murder, robbery, extortion. All this with your A-level exams a few days away. You have to leave, with your brother in prison, the police are coming for you. Your mother and father urge you to go. You flee.

Good qualifications are very important in your family. For you and your siblings, not having a degree was not an option. Accounting was your chosen subject for study at college. S, you decide to come to the UK to be a student. You were in a relationship for a year before you left. She was a student of clinical psychology you met in her final year at university. You had not yet started your studies. But you were a mature thinker by that time, and you both thought the age difference was not an issue, but the families did. The cultural barrier was huge in the relationship and against the norm. The reason you chose to become an accountant was so you might catch up with your girlfriend, and her professional career as a lawyer. Two years after you came to the UK you broke up.

So S, you start to explain your 'new life' as you move to the UK, the period from about 2008 to 2017 when you claimed asylum. You picked up on fees being cheaper at some colleges, you apply to the college you want to go to and receive a three-and-a-half-year visa. You arrive in the UK to find you've signed up to a 'visa college'. These 'colleges' are places where there are no classes. You were expecting the same level of education as in a university. There was no teaching at all, and you'd paid your tuition fees for the whole year. You wasted six months chasing the college for the education you'd signed up for and were never going to receive. You lose a year, and you lose your money. You sign up with a new college for the next academic year.

Happily, the first few years are good, you work hard at your study. You're doing well. You have friends who had arrived six months, a year before, and you're living in London. You live near the 'gherkin' building and use that as your navigation point, but still get lost when you get off the bus. London is so disorientating! It took several years to feel comfortable.

Language was not a barrier, but accommodation was a challenge – the college said it would provide a room, but you ended up looking for yourself. And your parents were a great help, providing money for the first few months, but the situation your parents were in, the charges your brother was facing meant there were legal fees. They couldn't support you further. Resources were limited. There had been a lot of shocks, nothing was going according to plan – the college that didn't exist, there were a lot of plans that didn't work out. But the first year away in the UK was a thrill, a new environment, new surroundings, new challenges.

From the first day, it seemed living in the UK would come with a huge task, and that task was cooking. Cooking became the way you orientated yourself with the city – a 2am trip to Tesco Extra, where you could find all the ingredients, opened up a new world to you. It kept you occupied. But finding work was a struggle. You moved to Purley where the rent was cheaper and started your college course in 2008. You'd take the bus an hour and a half to Borough each way, later realising how much time you were wasting, but it seemed normal. All normal. Where you came from a twelve-hour bus trip was not unusual, so an hour and a half seemed good! You worked in an Indian restaurant. It was an easy job. You were hesitant to speak your native language there, as the resident community speaks a different dialect to the one you know, but despite that you were welcomed by your own community.

There were no problems, you had a visa extension, so there was no need to claim asylum. You were studying for your accountancy exams and your English qualification towards your degree. This is late 2013, and there is a national scandal about students faking their English exams. The Home Office starts revoking visas, left and right. Your exam centre is shut down before they issue your results, so you don't have the prerequisite to enter the university. The requirements for English qualifications have changed in the years since you've been living in the UK. The goalposts have shifted. A previously deregulated system for English proficiency gradually becomes a mechanism for policing overseas students. So, you can't apply to university.

The situation has deteriorated at home. You are framed for taking part in violence where someone is killed, despite you living across continents in another country! It is time for you to claim asylum.

S, you claim asylum. Before this you had made four student visa applications in 2014, but because you had no English proficiency exam result, they were rejected, despite being in the UK for several years and your English being very good. Year on year the situation gets worse back home. As the years pass, asylum becomes the only possibility. You haven't broken the law, you didn't earn a single penny dishonestly or without paying tax. You didn't work any extra hours even when you were asked. You never thought you would be detained. Ironically, you had already lived a life of a refugee without any positive gains. You hadn't seen your family for nine years except for your sister. S, your religion and your devotion to it has saved you many times and been your guide. From 2009 to 2014 you were a youth worker.

S, you attend a music event in 2017, where a disturbance takes place, the police intervene and you are taken into custody. You are detained at various times over six months and threatened with deportation. You apply for humanitarian leave to remain through a human rights application with a choice of a discretionary application or the asylum application. The first detention was for fourteen days in June 2017 and a big shock. You thought detention was for people who had broken the law, had worked illegally. Others were put on signing conditions and attended reporting centres all around the country. These were new conditions. You get a lawyer who manages to secure your release. But this has already triggered trauma, as you were previously arrested in 2008 just after you had arrived in the country, by a police officer who said 'you have the misfortune of looking like someone else'.

It was a complex process to get out of the first fourteen-day detention, but you had a good advisor and a friend on the outside who helped you, and gave you a permanent secure address for official correspondence.

But this wasn't the end of detention. 2018 sees you detained for four months. And then again for three weeks a month later. S, you become hardened to it, braced. You want to make another submission of evidence, but the authorities detain you to block your action. S, you know of no one who has had a successful appeal, so things are looking bleak. Appeals are turned down usually within a day, but certainly no longer than a week. S, you receive a 'removal direction,' which means you have a month and a half. You have had to report every two weeks, and never missed an appointment, except when you were ill. To make a new submission you have to make an appointment to go to the Liverpool office to physically make the submission.

Before this, due to ill health, you couldn't attend the appointment in Liverpool and it was argued there was nothing to stop your removal. You have to go to your removals interview on your own without legal support, because you can't prove you need legal aid. There is the screening interview and the substantial interview, which are usually separate, but yours were run together. This takes place in 2017, and then you are called again in 2018. The interviews were six hours long.

In 2019, S, you are detained and you make an application to remain. It is rejected within a day. You receive a removal direction which is a month and a half from the date you said you intended to make a further submission. The rules seem to change weekly, the lawyers make money. Your solicitor tells you that any application to remain which you make in that period the authorities will want to refuse. And if you have a judicial review in this period it will override or defer the removal direction. This process means you cannot apply for bail for a month, so the process lengthens your detention. To gain bail you would need somewhere to stay and a financial guarantor. This can take months, when you have weeks. Often guarantors are immigrants themselves and would be scared of coming near a detention centre. You are fortunate – your guarantor has sufficient funds, your lawyer is a good one and you have your paperwork in order. You decide to delay the application by a month to delay the process and the removal direction.

Your further submission is a failure because you have no access to the internet. Your lack of access to online sources is not mentioned in your claim, so you appeal, and have evidence from the internet of your involvement in the party at home from their web pages. At the time the importance of this kind of evidence was not made clear to you; although you are involved on social media with the party. Because this evidence is missing, the judge claims that your association with the party can only be proved from decades ago, and therefore no one would see you as involved with the party now. Your counter-argument includes the torture of your brother, you had given reports of this and pictures to the Home Office, which they had lost. You don't meet your lawyer until the morning of the hearing, and she decides not to include your online involvement with the party at home, or in London. This evidence is not submitted.

S, you have no access to the internet in the detention centre, so it is very difficult for you to access your personal accounts where correspondence and your online presence would show how active you presently are in the party. On this, your further submission hinges. You manage to get some of the pages, by getting a friend to log into your social media accounts. He finds you have 252 posts, which you need to screen grab and authorise to go 'live' on the party's web page, thus proving your close connection to the party. There were letters of reference and pictures – all of this adds up to evidence of your activism since 2017. There are 100 pages of screenshots.

But you are told by the authorities in the UK not to do this, as you are going to be deported. So, the activities which have caused you to seek asylum you are asked to stop, which will help the Home Office facilitate your deportation, and yet are also proof of your current activity required for you to attain the status of leave to remain! It is a Catch-22 situation. Nevertheless, you are accused of getting involved in these activities to avoid deportation.

Because of a discrepancy between dates on the printout and some of your evidence, the judge does not allow the appeal. Your deportation is set for Bank Holiday Monday. A ticket is issued. You ask, 'what have I done to myself?' The Friday before the Bank Holiday your lawyer files for a sealed judicial review. She sends you a copy. But Saturday, Sunday, Monday, all the offices are closed. On Saturday morning, you are called by Immigration at the Detention Centre, they confirm your ticket for Monday. You say you have a filed judicial review, they say there is nothing on the computer system, they ask do you have a sealed judicial review, which you don't have, because you can't get to access the computer rooms because everything gets shut up four times a day so staff can carry out headcounts in the deportation centre. You get to the library, eventually, and you download the copy of the sealed judicial review and hand it to the immigration officer. You still have the ticket for Monday, but then receive a call on the Sunday to say the ticket has been deferred. You are hugely relieved, elated even. You ready yourself for release. You'd been there three months.

Then, in 2019, you are detained again. Your appeal had been unsuccessful. One of the reasons why it had been unsuccessful was that your status as an activist with a serious sentence hanging over you was seen by the court as equal to the status of your mother, an active professional sympathetic to the cause. The argument goes: if she is safe then so are you. But there were further letters of reference which had come in after your solicitors submit evidence for your appeal. They hadn't made them part of your further submission.

The next stage is the court of appeal. You carry on reporting and inevitably are brought back to the detention centre. This place is big, like a prison. You are locked up four times a day, you stay in your own cell, the toilet is there too. There are fewer facilities, libraries and access to the internet. Drugs are being sold, people smoke, use e-cigarettes. This was more a place for people who had served a sentence.

And now, because of the lockdown due to COVID-19, you do not have to report to fulfil your bail conditions. The Home Office calls you. Your bail conditions have remained the same ever since.

S, how you think has drastically changed after detention. Every reporting event is like a trauma and you have suffered depression since 2018. You only opened up to your doctor about this last year. You were a binge drinker at times. In detention, you thought the first days were the hardest, but then realised it was the days leading up to removal that were worse. The detention officials toy with people till the very last minute. Sometimes they take people to the airport and bring them back so the person gives up hope. They frustrate the bail process in every way they can. Removal directions are the most effective way to erode your morale. Every time you have been detained you have seen multiple suicide attempts. During your first detention you dislocated your shoulder, playing basketball with an officer. You didn't get adequate treatment for two weeks and you still suffer from that shoulder injury. In two separate detentions you broke your glasses, you were without your glasses for 60 days.

You talk, emotionally now, about the first day you came out of detention; you didn't want to walk out in public and went back home within ten minutes. You don't go out, even though you can now. You keep many of the details of your struggle a secret from your family – being separated for ten years from them is bad enough, and enough of a worry.

Somehow, throughout this process S, you became a chef! Way back when you started working in the Indian restaurant you saw a different way of cooking. You worked in other jobs in hotels and used different cuisines. It is not a respectable profession where you come from, and gastronomy has not developed very far. Over the years, you have managed to work as an assistant to some very well-respected chefs, one who worked for the Roux brothers. By chance you started working in a bank's restaurant in the city – it was the only way you could get to work close to the financial sector. You were trying to get a clerical or assistant role in the bank. One of the PA's in the bank where you were a chef really liked you. She left the job and gave you her number, and she wanted to meet. But your confidence was broken by then, after the first detention.

You had the required skills for cooking: you knew about ingredients and you knew how they relate to each other in dishes. To begin with, in 2009, you thought it was something you wanted to do part-time, a stop-gap, not your destiny. It has gradually become your profession, and you speak with real enthusiasm about it, in a way you don't about accounting. Your passion for cooking started after your time as a student had come to an end and your troubles had begun. You are interested in the logistics of cooking, the supply chain, the origins of the ingredient, consumer expectations – how it happens, the business side of food. Initially, you were working to pay the bills. But things changed when you began your job at the bank, where you were working for some renowned chefs. After a year you were offered an apprenticeship, but you turned this down, because your hours of employment are restricted to 20 per week.

S, you are taken under the wing of the head chef at the bank, and you see that this could be a profession that could work for you. As a chef you command respect, it's creative and it can be well paid. The training you have received is good and helps you along the way. You are consulted by a friend who is setting up a restaurant outside London about how you might run the business, as well as things you have learned in a Michelin-starred restaurant, such as plating skills, or how to cater to 50 people and maintain the quality of the food served. It's about maintaining a certain standard. You have also learnt about the business side of cooking, working with suppliers, and other skills. Your ambition is to open a restaurant someday.

You now work for a community food hub, where you use food close to the expiry date. S, you have developed the skills and art of cooking, and you have experience and training in finance – an unusual combination. And you know how restaurants operate financially, how to build relationships with suppliers and customers. This kind of overview is the difference between a chef and a cook. You like fusion cooking because you are a fusion yourself, in life. Still some recipes are authentic and better that way, and some you make from memory. You are familiar with British and European cooking and now want to work with other styles from around the world to create fusion elements in your repertoire. So, you've worked without spices as well as with the more European style of simple flavours from fresh herbs. The secret is to cook to the palate of the customer. These possibilities have given you great confidence.

S, you are in the process of opening a free community food hub in East London during the COVID-19 crisis. The idea is to turn surplus food into something beautiful and appetising. You want to open twice a month, then move to two days a week, and once you understand the business (social media, advertisement, publicity, funding) you want to open a pay-as-you-can-afford restaurant – where the needy and homeless get to eat for free.

The Delivery Person's Tale

as told by

HH

I WAS BORN IN the late 80s in Dakar, Senegal. My parents' families were both from Lebanon, although my mum was also born in Senegal, like me. Why Senegal? I can't tell you exactly why, but I can tell you about Lebanon. Lebanon is a small country whose structure has been arranged along ethnic lines since its foundation. In order to control and maintain balance, the constitution was formed to keep the people divided, not to unite them. Every minority will have a leader and their people follow them like sheep. A Muslim, a Christian, a Druze will each have to live in their own part of the country where their beliefs are in the majority. Each will only have one leader to vote for, who represents their faith.

Lebanon had many wars: wars with every neighbour, fifteen years of civil war that divided its people and left the whole population with hatred and scars, an ongoing war with Israel since the invasion of 1982. I never questioned my grandparents' decision to flee somewhere else. Both my mother's and my father's families have lived in Senegal for three generations. Both families integrated quickly and, being good at business, established a prosperous life within a few years. For my part, being born in Senegal was already a gift in itself, something that I couldn't possibly appreciate until I had seen more of the world myself.

My siblings and I were raised in an African way. We were looked after by maids. Yes, 'maids', I said it right, no? It might sound elitist to some, and I completely understand, but having a maid in Senegal is something very common. Senegalese locals also have maids; many people can afford a maid to help them clean the house, do the laundry and, in some cases like ours, help raise the children. Both my parents worked all the time and so left us with two local women full of devotion and love, Rama and Maimouna. For my first two years, I was tied to Rama's back with a large cloth while she was doing house duties: dishes, mopping, laundry and so on, till the end of the day.

As we got older, my parents decided to enrol us in a French school. Being born Muslim, and living in a Muslim majority country, did not stop me from going to Christian schools. On the contrary, since birth I was expected to respect others, accept them no matter what they looked like or what they believed in. We are human before all else, and we are born equal. French became my mother tongue since the official language in Senegal is French. Arabic was my second language. Then Wolof, of course, the dialect of the capital where I was raised, and the language of Rama and Maimouna. In the 90s, the Lebanese community was quite prominent in Dakar, with 25,000 Lebanese already doing business and living there, just like us.

> Mr HH, a dual Lebanese and Senegalese citizen, was born in Dakar to Lebanese parents who had migrated to Senegal for business. Before the applicant's birth, his father had started a company, with two partner brothers. The company was active in the sectors of aluminium, glass and the production of doors and windows. At its height, it employed 60 to 70 employees. Mr HH – a shiite muslim like his family, albeit non-practising – attended school until 2006. At that time, when the war ended in Lebanon, the family returned, because the grandparents lived there and were old and needed care.

Suddenly we found ourselves living in Lebanon; for family reasons, my dad shifted everything there. Lebanon, for all of us, was very challenging; yes, it was our country, but at the same time, no! We could not easily integrate. Due to our lack of Arabic, and our French mother tongue, we were like strangers. Unlike us, the people of Lebanon had lived through almost 40 years of war. They had been raised in war and division and, sadly, they were geographically, politically and religiously divided.

As for us, our education had been very different. Our way of living was not the same at all. We could not understand the mess in the country, and we were ostracised, seen as strangers in our homeland. My stay in Lebanon was quite short.

> The applicant's father bought a house in Beirut. After some months, he received a job offer which involved buying a share of the P Company that would open a branch in Alexandria of Egypt. It was a food company founded by Lebanese citizens and based in Australia.

In the summer of 2006, my father wanted to invest in a factory located in Egypt, to be a shareholder in this Australian-Lebanese factory. I was almost at the end of my high school studies when I decided to follow my father and go live in Egypt. Knowing the importance of his investment, I could not ignore it! I wanted to follow in my father's footsteps.

Everything was new to me. I didn't know the country, nor any of the new people surrounding me. But I bonded right away with most of them. I won't deny it and it was no secret. It's just that they were like us. What do I mean? They grew up, like us, in Senegal. They could also speak Wolof, French and Arabic, of course. The only difference was that they had lived in Australia for around fifteen years. This Lebanese-Australian family was quite big and, having the old Arab mentalities, they used to decide everything in the extended family community, and everyone obeyed the elder brother.

As time passed, being surrounded by this large, welcoming family, I grew close to the youngest sister. She was my age. The attraction was mutual. We could understand each other with just the blink of an eye. We fell in love.

> The applicant's father – who had obtained severance pay for his share of SM where he had also worked for 25 years – invested US$ 1,100,000 in the P Company, corresponding to 30% of the company's value. Therefore, Mr HH moved to Egypt and attended the French school in Alexandria where he met a nineteen-year-old woman named N, a family member of his father's Lebanese business partners, with whom he started a relationship.

From the very start, we decided to keep our love hidden from others. She asked me to do so knowing the mentality of her family, especially the elder brother. As I said, the Lebanese, most of them at least, focus too much on ethnic differences.

What did it have to do with us? Actually, everything. One family was Shiite and the other Sunni. Both are Muslim, of course, and there shouldn't have been a problem. According to Islam, even marrying a Christian or a Jew is also allowed under certain conditions. But when my relationship, or secret love, with this family's youngest daughter was exposed, a convocation was held, led by the eldest brother (the family boss), and they decided to ban us from seeing each other. They also confiscated her cell phone. Love was not allowed. Acting radically and extremely, her family took a stand based on ethnic difference. The union between Sunni and Shiite was not accepted.

I found a way to pass her a mobile phone so we could talk, at least, and stay in touch. But our precious moments together were about to end. Having lived so closely with her family for almost six months, especially in light of these events, my parents understood better than I could what kind of people they were dealing with. I was so in love that I couldn't see what my parents saw, nor understand.

My father was almost done with the paperwork by then; Egyptian procedures were very slow. Meanwhile, the money had disappeared from the company account. They diverted it somewhere without informing my father. They found some semi-legal way to do it, keeping my dad distracted with administrative paperwork, plus the pressure of my own situation with the girl. In the end, my dad could not trace his investment.

In fact, the factory was never built. Only a piece of land with nothing on it was owned by the company. The elder brother was always trying to hide the fraud by finding some legal excuses to justify the delay in the factory's construction. Doing his own research, my father discovered that the elder brother had fled Australia because of a very high number of similar fraud cases. On learning this, my father confronted them and exposed their behaviour in one of the project meetings. The tension grew greater than ever. The two families were at war now. Only a spark was missing. And here I came in with a most unexpected move.

Honestly, it was not my idea, but hers. I was more focused on the events surrounding us, but I could not deny my heart. How could I? I was so young and very much in love. We decided to flee to Thailand. A very bold move from both of us.

After a few months, the woman's family, who are Sunni Muslims, discovered the relationship and forbade her to go on with it, both because of their young age and due to their different faiths. For this reason, in 2007 the couple decided to move to Thailand where a friend of Mr HH's lived. Having paid about US$ 100, the applicant obtained a one-month tourist visa at the Thai Embassy in Cairo, while the woman did not meet any bureaucratic difficulty thanks to her French citizenship.

We chose Thailand because it was cheap and I had a contact there. So we had someone to guide us a little bit on our arrival, to be by our side. It took me two weeks to get my visa before landing in Bangkok. Both of us agreed to start a new chapter, and forget the hard moments in Egypt. United alone, in a new country with new beginnings, we thought love had conquered all.

Thailand was amazing in many ways and a very beautiful country. Shortly after our arrival, via my contact, we found a home in Phitsanulok in the north of the country. Then, for me, came the paperwork required if I wanted to live in Thailand – another challenge. For her, it was easy, since she was a French citizen. I renewed my tourist visa to stay in Thailand a couple of times. We were leading a wonderful life, not even wondering what was going on in Egypt. As far as I can recall, we enjoyed around eight months of serenity, like heaven on earth. But in order to stay in Thailand, I had to be granted a permit of stay. One of the conditions was to deposit an amount of $60,000 in the national bank of Thailand for at least three months.

As for the families, our running away led to even greater conflict. To be precise, just a few days after we left Egypt, the elder brother had attacked our home. By the end, everything was mixed together: business, religion, love. It was them blackmailing us: we would return their daughter and they'd return the money!

We already knew that the money would never come back, not without the authorities intervening. After making some complaints and official statements, my family went back to Lebanon once and for all.

Having learned of the escape, the woman's family retaliated against Mr HH's family members. In addition to threats and physical assaults against the applicant's father and brother, they reduced the father's shares in the company to 8%. The father refused to sign the contract being imposed on him asking, without success, for the restitution of the money he had invested. He also filed a complaint to the Egyptian judicial authorities in Alexandria, but without success.

My dad agreed to lend me the amount required for my three-year business permit of stay. I was missing some documents to open a local bank account, and due to heavy charges at the currency exchange, my father decided to visit me and bring the money by hand. Living nine hours' drive from the capital, I left a day before he arrived in order to meet him at the airport.

It was Friday afternoon when we arrived back home. My dad stayed in Phitsanulok for three days. On the Monday, we had to go to the Lebanese consulate, back in the capital, and to the national bank to prepare the account. On Monday at 5am, we took the road back to Bangkok. It could take up to 48 hours for us to clear the paperwork, so we allowed for 72. Of course, I kept the money safe at home before going to the hotel in Bangkok. On the first day, we finished our work at the consulate, but since we were very tired, we decided to go back to Phitsanulok the following morning. We took the road after a late breakfast, around 11am.

While parking the car in front of my home, my dad asked me why everything was turned off, no lights? It was around 9pm, she knew we were arriving, she couldn't possibly be asleep.

That evening was unlike any other. As I entered the room I had a strange feeling. At first, I was scared something had happened to her, but as I turned on the lights, my heartbeat increased, then I started to get a picture. I wasn't completely sure, and I was praying to be wrong. I just had the feeling that she had found the money, taken it and disappeared. Yeah, my worst nightmare was unfolding...

Meanwhile, Mr HH renewed his monthly visa twice (which is the maximum allowed stay according to the local legislation) in the offices of Thailand police at the border of Cambodia and Laos. Each time he was requested a bank deposit of US$60,000 secured for

> three months. Having been given the money by his
> father who went to visit him, the applicant kept it
> inside the house he was renting with his girlfriend. On
> returning home [...], Mr HH found that the girlfriend
> had disappeared with the money. After about ten days,
> he was forced to go back to Lebanon.

She knew that my father was bringing money, and she knew
that I had hidden it at home. I tried to be smart for once, so I
divided the money in two: one part hidden from her, the
second I told her where it was. But 36 hours was long enough
for her to turn the house upside down and find all of it. She
took all $60,000, my only access to a permit of stay, and, above
all that, our savings too. I can't find the words to explain my
feelings at that moment. I was betrayed in all possible ways. I
didn't know where to start. All I knew was that I was the one
to blame. I was in shock.

My father was so worried about me and tried many times
to make me change my mind, but it was impossible to stay, so
we left Thailand for good.

> Informed of his return, the family members of the
> father's business partners – who punished N's escape by
> beating her – asked the applicant's family to meet.
> Although Mr HH was against it – as he was afraid of
> possible violence – his father accepted the invitation,
> hoping to have at least part of his invested money back.
> The meeting began civilly but progressively deteriorated,
> to the point of an actual physical assault on Mr HH –
> who was subsequently hospitalised for some days due
> to the injuries he sustained – while his father reported
> the incident to the authorities to little effect.

For almost a year, life got back to normal, except for the odd
phone call from the elders back in Egypt, threatening and
blackmailing us. But the story was far from over, even if my

ex-girlfriend was back with her family along with the money. As for me, I already had a new life in Lebanon, which I was by and large enjoying.

One Thursday evening, just after sunset, I went to the bakery. I did this most days – only this time was different. The sequence of events happened so fast that I could not see the whole picture. It was very dark and, just before arriving at my destination, I noticed two people walking toward me and took them to be ordinary pedestrians. In a moment I was surrounded, and I could not understand what was going on. A few hours later, I woke up in the hospital with many small injuries. All I remembered was that the guy on my left had said the name of the woman before hitting me with something across my face. Then I went blank, everything happened so fast. My family and I understood that we should not underestimate the anger of the elders in Egypt.

> Having resumed his studies and graduated from high school, Mr HH was again the victim of an ambush by two unknown persons in Beirut. They approached him one evening on a motorcycle, while he was parking his car. He was verbally intimidated by a series of statements about his relationship with N and was hit on his head with the butt of a weapon, fainting as a result of the blows he received.

A few days later, we received a phone call from the elders, confirming the plot against me that night. They were proud of what they had done. I had to plan for a safer life, far from all these meaningless problems and people. Again, I had to make a new start, a new life, a new home. Running away once and for all was a good solution. So, I decided to go back to Senegal where I would feel at home and safe. Senegal! My country! My home!

> Once recovered after a period of hospitalisation, the applicant made up his mind to move to Senegal where

he started working, first, in the company of a distant relative of his, located about 15 kilometres from the centre of Dakar, then, in a hotel in the city centre and, lastly, as the Manager of a Total Senegal filling station.

In less than a week, I was already settled and working for a fish factory. A few months later, I got a good position in a plastic factory located far from the capital. I took the opportunity with both hands. I was happy working there and finally had some peace of mind. Going back to Senegal was by far the best decision I had made in many years. The country itself was a healing ground. I reunited with friends, I was independent. What more could I ask from life?

After a couple of years working for the plastic factory, a new opportunity presented itself. This time we are talking about certain heaven on earth! You see, many people worked for hotels, but very few of them could get the job that I did. I lived in a hotel room at the beach of Ngor in Dakar, with access to all kind of services that a 4-star hotel can provide: room service, swimming pool, gym, sea, boat rides... all for free. And the food! Ah, the food was so nice! Eating in the restaurant every day, at the buffet or the pizzeria in the hotel, unlimited access to the hotel kitchen. I had to work for nine hours a day, five days a week and that was it. My job was not so hard, I liked it and appreciated every moment in the hotel. A few months later I even got a car for work purposes and personal use. Two of my friends had a similar job to mine in the same hotel and also lived there. One of them, Bilal, was always there for me. Life was more than kind to me during this time.

Above all, I had the privilege of that sublime moment most mornings: watching the sun rise from under the horizon. The reflection of the orange sky on the tides, bare feet on the dry golden sand, surrounded with palm trees, feeling in each and every breath the fresh morning breeze, the sound of the waves mixed with the birds' morning chant. I could feel the ecstasy in every sip of my espresso.

Five years had passed since the incident in Thailand. I had almost forgotten about it. That was just the past, the woman, the money, all of it. In Senegal, I liked to go fishing and would go once a week or so. Sitting on a docking bridge, feet in the water, face towards the horizon, I could peacefully enjoy my hobby.

Except that 2014 was about to end. I woke up in the hospital. I could remember nothing. The doctor was stitching my head. That's when I woke, in pain and in shock.

Even in Senegal, Mr HH feared further retaliation because some of the girl's relatives lived there. In fact, in 2014, while he was fishing on the beach around sunset, he was knocked unconscious by unknown people. When he regained consciousness, he found that he was bleeding, although nothing had been taken from him (wallet, mobile phone, personal effects).

The morning after, my family in Lebanon received a phone call from a relative of the elders in Egypt, happily taking responsibility for this act of revenge. Don't forget that they grew up like me in Senegal and lived in Dakar for many years. They could get to me even here if they wanted to, that was clear.

As it happened, these elders wanted me to go back to Egypt, ask for forgiveness, and take their sister's hand in marriage in the proper, religious way. This was the condition. For them, restoring pride and dignity was the only solution. Then later on we could talk about the whole fraud situation. If not, I would not have peace for the rest of my life. You can see their mentality now. I will let you judge.

Once again, I was in retreat. I went back to live at a friend's place, near a factory in Dakar's industrial zone. For my own safety, I had to remain hidden. I lived like a ghost for many months, waiting for the right opportunity. I did not know what it would be, and I couldn't make any decision. I was just patient, very patient until the right opportunity arrived. This was my shot! My one and only shot!

I learned of a way to get into Europe – an illegal way, even though I was the holder of two passports, Lebanese and Senegalese. I seized the opportunity of the wave of Syrian immigrants to arrive in Italy. But how?

> He contacted his family, in particular his mother, who urged him not to go back to Lebanon for his own safety. After a few months hiding at a friend's place in the industrial area of Dakar, on 25 September 2015, Mr HH left Senegal by plane going first to Lebanon and then Turkey. He arrived in Greece by boat and, around mid-October 2015, he finally succeeded in reaching Italy by sea onboard a tourist vessel. He had paid about 6,000 euros for each journey.

Taking a ticket to Lebanon was just like booking a train ticket, no need for paperwork, and from Lebanon to Turkey it was the same, I could just take a ticket and go. But the smugglers in Turkey use the Mediterranean Sea to cross to Europe. So then came another aspect of life.

Putting your life in danger just to cross a border is not easy. First of all, we were dealing with smugglers, very dangerous people. They could kill you for any reason. You mean nothing to them, only the two or three thousand euros they will get. And second: there is the sea crossing. Crossing the sea is hard, especially if it is at night and the equipment, including the boat, are not fit for such use. It was extremely dangerous for some.

Everything was arranged and I was set to arrive in Italy 72 hours from the departure time. Italy was my destination just because I had a friend studying there. I paid around three times what other people paid to cross the sea. The smugglers offered different packages and I took the most expensive one, including private boats, higher safety, higher comfort and higher stealth. These people are professionals.

Having transited through Greece for a night, and with

some delay, I finally arrived at the Italian coast of Puglia. I arrived safe and undetected; I had achieved my first goal! To be honest, I didn't know what was waiting for me, but still I had my own ideas. Of course, if you decide to leave everything behind and start a new life, you need some kind of plan.

Many outsiders have different expectations of Europe before they arrive. Some want to be rich in a year, others to be married in a month, and so on. My idea was quite different; I just needed to start a new life in peace. Having a high school degree and speaking four languages fluently gave me some confidence; I was not here to depend on a system, or exploit it. I started the asylum procedure. It was the end of 2015.

My approach as an asylum seeker was a little different to others. I immediately lived with my friend and paid for a bed in a double room with students. I was not in a camp and have not, to this day, taken any aid from the government, not even a bus ticket. I had financial support from my family, and my friend to guide me. My integration into Italian society was smooth. Having a Latin-based mother tongue, Italian was not so strange or hard; on the contrary, it was easy, and I liked it.

My first hearing took place around a year and a half after I applied. At this point, the Territorial Commission for Asylum Determination considers two aspects: your story, and your integration into the country.

On 23 January 2017, the applicant's case was heard at the Territorial Commission for Asylum Determination of Turin. Come the decision date of 9 June 2017, as notified on 11 July 2017, the Commission decided to reject his application for refugee status (Documents 1 and 2).

'No actors of persecution can be reasonably identified in Senegal, the country of origin of the applicant, that could satisfy the condition set forth by the Geneva Convention of 1951 to qualify as a refugee.'[1]

For some reason, my story was not convincing. As for my prospects of integration, I was quite sure they would seem positive since I'm well educated, adaptable and speak four languages. I have never been so wrong in my life!

Depending financially on my family was a big mistake for the Territorial Commission for Asylum Determination. You see, to some it seemed that I didn't try to integrate since I did not look for a job. My case was dropped. The only option now was to hire a lawyer to file for a second appeal and, most importantly, to find a job.

My quest for work revealed the truth of what an asylum seeker has to face. I'm not talking about Italy only, but about most of the world, and I have travelled a lot! If you are without documents, sadly, you are often treated as less than human. You can't work properly – I will come back to that – you can't rent a home, can't own a car or drive. I faced and overcame many issues trying to find work, and still it was impossible. Being without a permit of stay, you face situations where you are not regarded as credible. Generally, people need some guarantees and are suspicious of asylum seekers. Some of them think that being an asylum seeker means you have done something bad and had to flee. I heard a lot of stories and faced many accusations. It was sad to discover that some people in Europe still think like this.

The only job I could find was with my roommate's help. He was a student working part-time at a restaurant. He vouched for me to the boss and so I got a job. My second hearing was about to come when I received a message from my lawyer telling me that it had been delayed six months due to some changes in the court.

What about my job? I had to work twelve hours a day for six days a week for 900 euros, sometimes less. My employer declared only 30 per cent of my work, but I had to work to the contract. In short, my salary was for 20 hours a week while I was doing around 60. It was very hard, but my boss was not unkind. Even so, he abused my situation with regards to my lack of documentation. He knew I needed that contract at all costs to get my permit of stay.

It would take a whole chapter to describe the horrors of being taken advantage of in this way, but this job was my only ticket to a brighter future. After three years, the second hearing was about to start, and this time I had a work contract and a B2 level degree from a public college under my belt.

Only the judge didn't even take a look at my integration into Italian society or my work but focused only on my story. This time, however, I brought evidence. I brought documentation of the complaint to the Egyptian authorities against the elders. This report was consistent of two parts, as well as the proof of the bank wiring, my dad's investment, and an official statement showing that the elders were wanted for fraud in Australia. But even this did nothing, really nothing. The judge could not see the link between my story and my dad's investment.

> The Court shares the argument of the Territorial Commission for Asylum Determination: 'No actors of persecution can be reasonably identified in Senegal, the country of origin of the applicant, that could satisfy the condition set forth by the Geneva Convention of 1951 to qualify as a refugee'. [...] Even assuming that the assailants are the former girlfriend's family members, one cannot claim that the Senegalese authorities are unable or unwilling to provide effective protection against attacks upon the applicant. This circumstance is prevailing and exempts us from ruling out the possibility that the applicant could also have accessed internal protection in Lebanon.[2]

My lawyer and I lost the case, so then it went to the higher court. I could not understand if I was cursed or if it was just my destiny.

Again, a full year passed before it went back to court, and obviously I had to keep my underpaid job because of the need for the contract – further opportunity for my boss to exploit me more, knowing my situation.

Finally, April 2020 was scheduled as my last hearing, and it was soon. As the year started, a new terror arose in the world, the one called COVID-19. Due to national lockdown, the hearing was again delayed for six months. In COVID times, in order to keep my job, I had to make more and more sacrifices. Instead of being a bartender, I had to work in the kitchen now, clean shrimps, clean dishes, fry the food. In the same shift, I was expected to make deliveries on my bicycle in the rain, and to clean and lock up at the end of the night. All of it with a smile on my face. It was getting harder and harder; I could not bear it anymore.

September 2020, in front of the court, I spoke in Italian to the judge with three years of paychecks in my hand. I hoped this time, surely, they would allow me a permit of stay. A few days after what I thought was my last audience, I was jobless. I hadn't been able take it anymore, and saw no more reason to continue making all those sacrifices, so I decided to leave my work. Another wrong decision, I guess.

The whole world drowned in a second wave of COVID-19 in November, and I was free from the old sacrifices, but also out of work. It was impossible, even for normal citizens, to find a new job in these conditions, so imagine what it was it was for those with no permit of stay? As for me, I was denied any COVID-19 financial aid due to reasons related to my last job, so in order to survive and pay my rent, I had to do deliveries on my bicycle across town.

Food delivery is quite well known in Europe, and you will find many Apps for it. Doing deliveries was not enough, so my sister took on the responsibility of paying my rent. She comes to visit me in Italy most years, supporting me a lot emotionally in many situations, and financially too. Her presence was vital in keeping me going.

Italy. This country has given me some seriously difficult times, but what a unique experience! I am living in a city full of asylum seekers and outsiders, from eastern Europeans to Arabs, Africans, Asians and more. I can communicate with most of them, and it is like a superpower for me. Sometimes the police used to stop me for sitting and talking with my Senegalese buddies in the parks during the summer. And the first question was always: how come you understand them? Most of the time that was the reason for police intervention – curiosity. It was very funny, sometimes, to see the reaction of others regarding my use of the language, how they felt it related to ethnicity, or to my skin colour.

I remember once, I was with my sister in Milano at Piazza Duomo, doing some shopping. We stopped at the Armani store to get some products. My sister was buying a gift for her fiancée, so we were talking and exchanging opinions. Of course, the saleswoman was near us. My sister and I speak French to each other though some Arabic comes out sometimes. But with the woman standing there, we spoke in Italian and English. We completely blew her mind, as she told us. Later on, she asked us where we came from and how we were fluent in so many languages. What a proud feeling! If only she knew that I had no permit of stay and that I could not even get a normal job as a sales assistant, like her, even with my talents!

These days, what happened in Thailand is only a dark memory where no sunlight reaches and I hope life remains like it is. Staying focused, looking straight ahead. I really hope to see the light at the end of this dark tunnel soon, to start a journey for a better life.

Since his arrival in Italy (October 2015), the applicant has committed himself to learning Italian (such that, when he appeared in Court, he demonstrated that he had mastered it perfectly) and has taken up work which, at present, as a sign of progress and positive inclusion, is permanent and allows him to be economically self-supporting including being to house himself […]. The personal circumstances, as established, even though different from most other cases of international protection, are, in the Court's opinion, nonetheless sufficient to establish, at least on provisional and hypothetical bases, that Mr HH, if repatriated, would not enjoy objective nor subjective prospects of a decent life, first, because he would be deprived of family or emotional relations, having categorically broken all connections with the countries of origin many years ago in contrast to his present situation in which he is an active and useful part of the country that has welcomed him.[3]

Notes

1. Territorial Commission for Asylum Determination, Decision of 9 June 2017, published on 11 July 2017.
2. First instance Court decision of 18 June 2019, published on 28 June 2019.
3. Court of Appeal decision of 22 December 2020, published on 3 March 2021.

The Advocate's Tale

as told by

JB

My name is JB and this is my story.

I was recognised as a refugee in 2015, here in the United Kingdom. I arrived in the UK in 2012 and I was detained on the very day I applied for my asylum, without being given a clear reason why, and without being told how long I would be held for. All they told me was, 'We are taking you to a safe place where we shall work on your case very quickly.' Of course, as I later found out, that wasn't the case. I was about to face something even worse than the persecution I was running away from back in my home country. Life in detention became the worst experience of my life.

Since being released from detention, I have made it my business to fight for my brothers and sisters who are still stuck in there with whatever little means I can. Not because I also passed through the same situation. Not because it's the right thing to do. Not because the whole system has failed us, rather than helped. And indeed, not because it's a waste of taxpayers' money. But simply because, as an asylum seeker, detention was the worst place I have ever been in my life, at a time when I needed help the most. It gives me nightmares knowing that another person has to go through the same experiences every day. But I believe we could put an end to these experiences, and this can only be achieved by putting an end to indefinite detention.

Put yourself in the shoes of those people fleeing their home country, seeking refuge here in the United Kingdom, or in neighbouring countries. Once you made it here you would expect to receive some sort of help or protection, right? Well, in my case it was the opposite. My experience in detention was worse than I can describe.

We were held under Class 'B' high security, locked in prison cells for long hours, treated as criminals, and sometimes even worse. For an extremely vulnerable person seeking refuge from persecution in his own country, this becomes a form of torture.

I remember a young man in the cell opposite mine who used to cry in pain to the officers every day and night. 'Please, officer, please, take me to the hospital. Or at least give me some medication, I am dying.' But all his crying fell on deaf ears. One day, when his cellmate rushed out of the cell in panic that he was actually dying, we had to go on strike so that he could get the attention he so badly needed. When he was eventually rushed to the hospital, after he couldn't talk anymore, we were so eager to find out what had happened to him, whether he was still alive or not. But we never heard a thing from him again. One of the men committed to our wing told us, in shock, that that sort of behaviour from the staff was not even common in the prison where he served a criminal sentence.

Winning your case in the Detention Fast Track system was close to impossible, as the great majority of the asylum cases were rejected, and so was mine. This didn't surprise me because it seemed that the entire structure of the Fast Track system was designed to result in the refusal of asylum claims, rather than a fair judgement on the vulnerable cases. Even though every solicitor who saw my case argued that it was strong, I only managed to fight my case and be granted asylum after I was released.

Seeking medical help was a waste of time because we only had one doctor on each wing, who seemed to only ever prescribe paracetamol. After suffering from diarrhoea twice, I went to the doctor and asked him why I was denied medication even though it was prescribed to me. This is what he had to say: 'We fear people could take an overdose. Sorry, I can't give it to you.' But I wasn't allowed to take it in his presence either, so I wondered why he was there at all.

Eating anything was only possible with a really strong motivation to try. Not because we didn't want to, but because we were so depressed and traumatised by the whole situation in detention. Many of us went on hunger strike to express our despair towards the way we were treated, and to protest about being detained in the first place.

Having to witness people attempt suicide is itself a form of torture, leaving you hopeless and without the mental capacity to fight your own case. It really feels as if there is a deliberate attempt to crush your mentality.

This is only to mention a few aspects of detention. Somebody today might ask, has the situation actually changed for the better? I guess the answer to this million-dollar question is, No. These things still happen in detention today. And this is why we call for an end to detention. Especially now, because today we have Coronavirus. We don't know what tomorrow will bring.

It costs the Home Office about £96.66 per day to keep a detainee behind bars. And because of the appalling conditions and the many cases of unlawful detention, the Home Office has been challenged numerous times in the courts by charities like Detention Action. But of course, some cases go unanswered, like those of people who are unlawfully deported, and those who take their own lives or face very serious medical conditions under this system.

I hope we can see a better tomorrow and make a change once and for all by putting an end to indefinite detention.

The Prisoner's Tale

as told to

Christy Lefteri

I'VE NEVER MET LILY and she will be fifteen soon. Beautiful Lily, sweet Lily, with the silent voice. She does not speak but she is very intelligent.

I didn't want to meet her for the first time in detention, that would have been a really bad thing. Nobody wants to meet their daughter for the first time like that. It cements the stereotype. Black man in jail. This is not my family's tale. That's not how we live our lives.

The thing about the detention centre is that it suits them to segment people. On one side are those strictly with immigration issues and, on the other, people who are being deported because they have criminal pasts. I was put in this section when I got here, with the criminals, the hardened guys.

I didn't know that this was the case when I first arrived. I just thought this is what detention is like everywhere. After about a month, one of the immigration officers was going through my records and she said,

'Why are you here, in this wing, why are you in T Wing?'

I said, 'I don't know, I'm just here.'

She said, 'Yeah but you don't have a criminal record,'

'No, I don't have one.'

'Then you should not be here. You should be on the other side.'

Oddly enough, the security in this wing is comparable to a high security prison. It's a strange place to be: there are fights, there are people high on drugs. They take Black Mamba and Spice. Zombie drugs. Drugs that space you out, slow you down. You see people sprawled out. It's so bad that even the guys who are selling have learnt how to put people in the recovery position. They've been watching the emergency medical team when they come in, they watch them, and learn. I've seen lives being saved.

People come to T Wing clean. The thing about detention is this: you don't have a release date. They say that you're meant to spend a maximum of six months here and then you will have a review. That's not true. People spend years here. That... uncertainty. That... *where is my life going?*

This is all I knew: they were trying to deport me. I was constantly fighting an invisible enemy.

Once Friday passed, I relaxed. We all get weekly reports about how we've behaved and whether the Home Office has turned against us. If there is nothing negative in the letter, then you celebrate. I got to chill for two days, Saturday and Sunday. Come Monday, the fight started again.

You're not really in prison, but that's what it feels like. They lock your room at 9pm and open it at eight in the morning. You're in a cell for approximately twelve hours a day.

But the guys inside are saying to me, 'Now look, you're getting off. You're going to be free.'

I first came to the UK from X with my mother in 1998, when I was ten years old and she came for school. The government had a programme where they sent people to England. She studied Developmental Science and Rural Development because she wanted to work with NGOs. Back then, we stayed in Manchester.

The most startling thing was the cold. I was introduced to a game called rugby. When we played, my hands turned blue. I told the PE teacher that my hands had gone blue and he said to me,

'Okay, go home and run them under cold-ish water.'

And I thought to myself, 'If my hands are cold, why would I run them under cold water?' So, I ran them under hot water. And I screamed.

The next day he asked me, 'Did you run them under cold water or hot water?'

I smiled and I told him hot water.

He said, 'Was it painful?'

I told him, very painful!

I'd never experienced cold like that before. That's one of the longest memories I have of those early days. I was exposed to that really cold weather.

I was alone a lot.

In Manchester, at the time, it was so different from home. People kept to themselves. When we were kids, we just walked outside, friendships started from there. Parents weren't too worried about where their children were, they knew they were playing in the park with other children. Here I found that it wasn't the same. It's only when I moved to another area in Manchester that things were different. The majority of the kids were Pakistani and Indian – they were running helter-skelter there! I even learnt to play cricket!

By the time I was seventeen, I was a very good sportsman. You know, your typical jock, playing football. Everybody knows you because you play footy. Well, things were going on back home that I did not know about. My mother's younger brother died. But she didn't fill me in on what was happening. I just remember she was in pain because her brother died. But she never really let me know about everything, not even about the asylum application. I didn't know about that. She kept me in the dark. I was trying to play football when I was a teenager, trying to be as good as I could. I wanted to get a scholarship to play American college soccer. Lots of my friends tried out and eventually did go. But my mum's request for asylum was denied and we had to leave and go back to our country of exile.

Before we left, though, I had a relationship and that resulted in my daughter being born a year later. By that time, I was no longer there.

Beautiful Lily, sweet Lily, with the silent voice. I have seen photographs of her, had little conversations with her on Skype, where she smiled and said a few words – whatever she could manage. I've never held her in my arms and told her that she will be safe in this world – that I will keep her safe. A tale that every father tells.

Now the guys inside are saying to me, 'You're good to go. You're going to get off.'

It scares me that I have never met my daughter. The Home Office were using this against me. I told them, 'I have a family!' But in the report they gave me, they wrote things like:

Has no family ties.

That's one of the things that they always wrote:

Has no family ties to the UK, and therefore would abscond if he got bail to be out of detention.

The reason they were saying this is because Lily hadn't come to see me. But I didn't want my daughter to see me in here, like a prisoner. If she was to come in and prove that she is my daughter, maybe their report would have changed. But nobody wants to meet their daughter for the first time like that.

I would have probably chosen another place, maybe. Back home, you hear people call the UK a hostile environment.

From afar, when you hear about a hostile environment, and when you see what's going on with people like Trump and all these things, it's not easy to even think about coming to a place like this. It's… it's… it's… it's… Sometimes I am lost for words.

I am lost. I feel lost. But I came here for Lily. I would have gone somewhere friendlier, like South Africa, just as a friend of mine did. But if I went there, I would have been so far from my child.

A few months before I came back to the UK, my brother was stabbed. In the West, you will say *cousin*, but in my culture I call him my younger brother. It's a different way of viewing family altogether. It can't be compared. Apples and oranges.

He was stabbed in the neck and killed in a shopping mall in February. It was done in public, not in secret. Stabbed in the neck and people just walked away. Back home, we have capital punishment, but this guy murdered in the open and he's still free. This is tribal stuff. We're from X originally, but we always have tribal issues amongst ourselves.

Before coming here, I got interrogated by a government directorate. My grandmother had children with a prominent person, that person was one of the first members of parliament when my country was formed. He happens to be my grandfather. He was in power since 1966 and his son, my father, was subsequently also a member of parliament until recently. I have lots of family connections in politics as a result of that. I mentioned this to one of my bosses. I was a procurement officer in my country in the same region and he didn't know my past because my surname is different from my grandfather's, as my mother didn't get married to my father. I mentioned it once and after a month or so I got called in to be investigated for corruption and economic crime. Because they thought, 'Oh okay, this is a political connection,' that I might be giving kick-backs to my uncles and so forth. I stopped going on campaigns, I stopped being involved in certain things. If they know your family they know which way you lean politically. It's not about what you know, it's who you know.

I got a ticket, quite expensive, and went to Ireland, because I had no history there. I understood that I would have problems coming straight to the UK. I planned to go through Northern Ireland, to Scotland, and finally get to Manchester where my daughter was staying and claim asylum at a later stage. The guys back home who worked in immigration said, 'You don't know how it could go there, with the hostile environment in the UK. You just don't know.'

At this point in time, all I was thinking was that I had to see my daughter. As much as I was worrying about what was going on in my country, the only thing that really mattered was the idea of meeting my daughter.

I landed in Ireland. I spent a few days there and I came over through Northern Ireland and showed my passport. It was a strange thing. That's where I encountered problems, when I arrived in Scotland. The border police stopped me. They wouldn't let me in. They said, 'You've had previous immigration problems and therefore you have to go to a detention centre. And that's what we're going to do.'

So I spent a few hours in the police station. It was the first time I'd ever been in handcuffs.

I went to the detention centre in Glasgow. I was lost. I wanted to see Lily.

I told them, 'I want to see my daughter.'

They told me, 'We want to deport you.'

The food was a problem. After breakfast, I didn't feel like eating. I was just bloated the whole time. I don't know what was going on. You just eat because it's time to eat, not because you're hungry or you want to eat. You eat.

I asked my friend, 'What do they put in this food?'

He said, 'I feel the same way all the time.'

We shared rooms, sometimes in twos, sometimes in fours.

This guy was Congolese. His English was not so great. He was saying, 'My roommates are always bursting.'

I said, 'What do you mean your roommates are always bursting?'

What he meant was that they were farting.

We ate in the cafeteria. Dungavel is open, men and women in one place, grass, greenery. But then there's a point that you can't pass because you'll be approaching the fence and you're not meant to do that. Because they're watching you. They've got cameras watching you. Intensive security. Dogs. Guards walking around with dogs, checking the perimeter all the time. Sometimes they're showing you their presence, they're showing you that *we are here*. If anyone was to try to jump over *we are here*. It could turn negative quite quickly.

Apart from that the staff members were quite relaxed. It was okay, good library, lots of DVDs and things like that.

I was moved though. I was moved to London after three weeks, after I had my initial interview. Before the interview, they tried to deny me the right to apply for asylum, on the basis that I had applied before. But I was a minor then. They were going to send me back home, they booked the flight and everything and I said to them, 'If you're going to send me anywhere, send me somewhere else, not back there.'

My solicitor put through a judicial review to allow me to apply for my asylum. Technically, I'd never made an application on my own. I wasn't even eighteen when I left the country the first time.

So I had my interview, finally, and I was sent to London so that I could hopefully have a bail hearing. I remember being told by some of the guys in detention, 'Look mate, London is a different ballgame altogether.'

Here, I spend about twelve hours inside and then you're allowed to walk around in your particular wing. For three hours, maybe, you can go to the gym or something like that.

And if they allow you access to the church, you can go to church, depending on which day it is.

Someone died in detention. It was a guy from my church. Late at night, there was a loud crash and the people in the cells next door tried to get the attention of the guards. But the guards ignored them, they did not come. In the morning, the guards discovered him on the floor. They dragged him out and attempted to resuscitate him and the guy next door – very skinny guy from Sudan – he said to them,

'You guys must think you are Jesus Christ. You're trying to revive the dead. We know that he died yesterday. So there's no use trying to revive him for show.'

The guys that have been to jail said to me, 'Come on, don't let the system beat you down!'

But they are stronger. They know how to handle it more. Me, I've never considered criminality, I could never imagine being locked in a cell. In Glasgow, it was different. Although I still couldn't leave, at least they had this artificial way of making it look like you're not in a jail cell. This detention centre is a prison. They call it a detention centre, but it's a prison. It violates your mind because you have no way to know what is going to happen next. People know how to do *time*. You tell them, *six months, then you're free*. Here, anything can happen to you. Sometimes you can have an over-zealous case worker who is always against you, who turns the Home Office against you. Your dilemma is fighting the Home Office. The worst are the engagement officers – witches and crooks – they're the worst. They come in pretending to be good listeners, a listening ear, but in actual fact they are there to suss you out. You don't get to see your case worker, you just see the engagement officer. They tell you they don't have the power to do anything, they're only there to hear you out.

I ask, 'Are you going to hear me out, to speak on my behalf?'

They say, 'No.'

'So, if you're not speaking on my behalf, then I can only

assume that you are working against me.'

The other guys in detention told me that I shouldn't be meeting with my engagement officer. They said, 'that's the worst thing to do!'

For two months I was meeting with my engagement officer, not knowing that everyone else was not doing that. It was working against me. This is standard practice. The engagement officer will call you to arrange a meeting, and you ask them,

'Would you like to meet because you're coming to tell me that I'm going to be released?'

'No.'

'Then there's no point in us meeting.'

They're collecting information about you, making reports. If you get into a fight, if you play football and there's a bit of argy-bargy, you might find that when you go to your bail hearing something like that will pop up. And you think, 'Wait a minute... how did that get so far to arrive in the courtroom? How does the Home Office know about this one small thing?'

Beautiful Lily, sweet Lily, with the silent voice.

And now... now the guys inside are saying to me, 'Now look. You're getting out. You're good to go. You're going to get off.'

So, finally, things started to go well. I went to court again, in Bradford, to address what had happened before. I remember being there. My barrister and the Home Office barrister were talking about fish and chips in Ireland. It looked like they were having this conversation beforehand, they were talking about fish and chips in Ireland during my court case, just before the judge arrived. When the judge came in, my barrister stood up and spoke and then the Home Office barrister said to the judge,

'Look, there's nothing to argue here about how the previous judge carried out the case. She was wrong in the way she carried out the law and I'm not even going to argue against it.'

It was so badly done that the judge didn't even bother arguing – he just let it be. The detention process, that whole situation, that's how badly it can go for you. The court case lasted about three minutes. My barrister spoke for about two minutes, the judge for one, and that was all. Then a report came out two days later saying,

> We are going to start again from the beginning, and then we can move forward.

And that was just the beginning of another long process, waiting for my bail hearing, imagining my daughter like a bright star in the dark sky, urging me to keep going, to not give up.

So, this time, well, now I'm getting out. I know my way around London because I came many times when I lived in Manchester, once upon a time. If I get lost, I will find myself again. When you're taken to a bail hearing, you leave the way you entered. This time it's different; I'm not in a locked vehicle. I am *walking* out of detention. Through the massive, massive, massive gates. Like I said – high security. I cannot stop thinking about Lily. It's hard for me to believe that I will be meeting her soon. I will be staying with someone I know until I get accommodation sorted. I needed to be able to give them an address so I could get out. But, before anything else, I will be meeting Lily.

The thing about my daughter is that she's got a condition, social anxiety, she does not speak much. She's really intelligent. She suffers from extreme shyness and she is having counselling. She is no longer in your regular school. So, she goes through a lot. When I spoke to her mother on the phone, we made a point that when I first meet her, it's not going to be a Hollywood moment – you know, slow motion, slow music, me picking her up and twirling her around. Although that is exactly what I want to do!

I should be as calm as I can. Too much attention makes her

freeze. She gets sad because she's not able to interact like you and me. This puts a lot of pressure on her to do it, and she fails. Then she feels sad because she failed. But if you don't give her the opportunity to interact with you, she's sad because she feels left out.

So it's like a double-edged sword.

I have to be restrained when I give her a hug.

Beautiful Lily, sweet Lily, with the silent voice.

The sun is setting, but it's still a little bright out. I feel disorientated.

So I get on the bus.

Epilogue

AND NOW THEREFORE
This morning
We are at the season's edge
Where the swallows
And the house martins
Prepare to leave us
Turned
Towards the sun
And whereas the tree line
Waits
Burnt
In its image
We count the day's
Elements

Corn
For a friend
Because it shoulders
Our belonging
And where the ground has hardened
We count the morning's dew
For another
Who walked
One who witnessed rivers

And mountains
Turned back
Towards the water
As it were compelled
To choose

At the edge
This morning
Where the season dries
And alters
And the birds know
That a winter
Is coming in
And we know
As we watch
These are the days
Define us
Sky
Reached out
Therefore
Now
And

Afterword

The Walk

Refugee Tales is a walking project. Every summer since 2015 the project has set out on a large-scale public walk. The purpose of the walk is to call attention to the fact that the UK is the only country in Europe that detains people indefinitely under immigration rules. The project calls that fact out and it calls for detention to end. Detention is arbitrary and brutal and as the drive to decolonise our culture tells us, when as a society we finally acknowledge what we have done, those who have enforced immigration detention will surely be ashamed.

The walking community – Refugee Tales is nothing if not a walking community – varies and changes from walk to walk. Some people will have walked before. Some will be joining for the first time. Some will have recently been detained. Some will have been detained more than once, perhaps for months or years, and because the process is arbitrary will not know when it might happen again. Some, because of where they were born and happen to be living, will not be at risk of detention. Because make no mistake, and notwithstanding the fact that the rules are complicated and bewildering, when we detain people in the UK we do so on the basis of nationality and race.

As for the act of being on the walk, it is possible to say without fear of contradiction that the walking itself is a pleasure. Some people know the route – these walks are planned, not improvised – but for almost everybody the ground is new. It is also hard, which everybody finds out when they sleep on it, since the project spends the nights on the floors of churches and village halls. These spaces double as venues for the evening performances, when the stories eventually published as part of the Refugee Tales series are first heard. The stories are difficult, because the UK's system of detention is brutal, and for many people in the room they are a reminder of an experience they have had and might yet have again. And so, to lift the mood, each evening there is music, and where there is music the walkers of Refugee Tales dance. And then the next day the project walks again, committed again to ending detention, because what each story says, as it details the fabric of an individual life, is that we have to make a future in which people are not detained.

When Refugee Tales first walked in 2015, from the Immigration Removal Centre on the White Cliffs of Dover to the Immigration Removal Centres at Gatwick Airport, driven by the work of the Gatwick Detainees Welfare Group, there was no expectation that the walking would continue year after year. The power to detain had been on the statute book since the Immigration Act of 1971, but for much of that time had been relatively little used. In 1973, 95 people were detained indefinitely under immigration rules. By 1988 that figure had increased to 2166.[1] In 2015, over 32,000 people were indefinitely detained in the UK, with the longest known period of detention being nine years:[2] the case of a man from Somalia who was 'found' in Lincoln Prison by HM Chief Inspector of Prisons, abandoned to and by the system. You might think it would hardly need stating, but let's be clear: detention is a breach of a person's human rights. In case we were in any doubt about that, the authors of the *Universal Declaration of Human Rights* spelt it out for us. As Article 9 states: 'Nobody shall be subjected to arbitrary arrest, detention, or exile'. Surely it would be enough, Refugee Tales felt in 2015, to call attention to such a scandalous and escalating breach of human rights to trigger a process of political change. Except, of course, that in an age driven by the politics of sovereignty and narratives of nation, human rights are an inconvenient truth, and so for Refugee Tales, as for all groups calling for an end to detention, it has been necessary to keep walking, to dig in.

And so the walk has continued because the political objective has not yet been achieved, because still in the year ending March 2020, 23,075 people were detained.[3] We should notice that the number has come down somewhat from the historic high of 2015 and we should notice also that the time periods of detention have gradually reduced. Due to the relentless public pressure of a wide network of campaigning organisations and NGOs, and due to the extensive reporting that followed the Windrush Scandal – through which it became public knowledge that the Hostile Environment had extended its reach to people who had lived in the UK for many years – there has been a partial contraction of the detention estate. Such progress as this represents is incremental and the addiction to detention remains visibly strong. At the time of writing, recently arrived asylum seekers are being held in intolerable conditions in the former Napier Barracks in Folkestone, acutely vulnerable to COVID-19 and variously denied access to lawyers and general practitioners. It is also reported that the Home Secretary intends to open new detention centres (or spaces within existing detention centres) for women, in direct contradiction of the previously stated intention to end detention for women with the closure of Yarl's Wood. What the recent history of detention demonstrates is that it will never be enough to bring the numbers down. There has to be a change of law. To change the law will be to establish the primacy of human rights. It is for this reason that Refugee Tales continues to walk.

But this is not the only reason. There are, in fact, many reasons, not least that over several years and across many miles of walking, both on the large-scale summer walks and the intervening monthly gatherings, something like a mobile community has formed. As people have walked and as stories have been shared – whether as co-productions with writers, or as first-person testimonies, or, as is increasingly the case, in films directed by Ridy Wasolua shaped by his own experience of detention, or in conversation, or on WhatsApp, or in the Parliamentary Advocacy group led by people with lived experience of detention – the Refugee Tales project has come to a deepened understanding of the structures of hostility the UK sustains; the way in plain sight official processes isolate and dismantle human lives; the way, instead of welcome and refuge, what the UK continues to practice is an arbitrariness which cuts deep into any concept of human rights.

The Walking Inquiry

In 2017 the BBC programme Panorama staged an undercover investigation into the treatment of people held in detention at the Brook House Immigration Removal Centre at Gatwick Airport. As is the case with all so-called 'immigration removal centres' in the UK – centres where people are detained, detention centres – Brook House is privately run, by G4S at the time of the investigation, now by SERCO. Access to removal centres is difficult to arrange, whether by legal representatives or visitors' groups, and at any one time, given the arbitrariness of the processes, it will be hard to establish who is being held. Panorama gained entry by providing one of the detention centre staff with a hidden camera.[4] What the footage disclosed was a regime in which people detained were routinely abused, the defining moment being when a detention centre officer, on finding a person who had tried to strangle themselves in their cell, responded by placing his hands around the person's neck to finish the process off. It was an awful spectacle and, quite rightly (following repeated calls), the end of 2020 saw the beginning of a Public Inquiry into abuses at Brook House.

The purpose of the Inquiry, as its website states, is 'to investigate into and report on the decisions, actions and circumstances surrounding the mistreatment of detainees broadcast in the BBC Panorama programme "Undercover: Britain's Immigration Secrets" on 4 September 2017'. As the Inquiry's terms of reference state, '"Mistreatment" is used to refer to treatment that is contrary to Article 3 ECHR, namely to torture or to inhuman or degrading treatment or punishment.' As regards duration, the Inquiry's remit is strictly defined:

> For the purpose of the Inquiry, the term 'complainants' is used to refer to any individual who was detained at Brook House Immigration Removal Centre during the period 1 April 2017 to 31 August 2017 where there is credible evidence of mistreatment of that individual.

Refugee Tales welcomes the Brook House Inquiry, as it does any inquiry into the abuses of detention, and people associated with the project and with Gatwick Detainees Welfare Group are submitting evidence. What, as a project, we would draw attention to is the inquiry's scope, the restriction of its interest to the period 1 April 2017 to 31 August 2017. How is it possible, Refugee Tales asks, to separate out a specific period or context of abuse from a system which, in its arbitrariness and its indefiniteness, is abusive at its core? To which end, and in order to complement the findings of the Public Inquiry, and building on its own processes and collective experience, Refugee Tales has established a Walking Inquiry into Immigration Detention to amplify and extend the conversation.

The purpose of Refugee Tales' Walking Inquiry into Immigration Detention is to explore the human costs and societal implications of a system in which people are arbitrarily detained. The Inquiry has two methodological principles. First and foremost, its shape and direction is determined by people who have lived experience of detention. Second, its deliberations are shaped by the act of walking, by the exchanges and solidarity that come of walking together. The walking part has been difficult since, under lockdown, people have had to walk separately, staying in contact as they walked by social media and by phone. Through that fragmented process, however, the first stage of the Inquiry arrived at the following deliberately broad questions:

- What is it like to be detained?
- How are people detained
- What are the long-term impacts of detention?
- Why are people who have experienced detention not heard?
- How does detention damage society?
- What is our response?

Each month, from January 2021, the Walking Inquiry has considered one of these questions, with deliberation of each question led by a series of filmed submissions. The principal film each time was made by Ridy Wasolua, out of contributions from people who have experienced detention, with accompanying films from lawyers, detention visitors, academics, health professionals and others with relevant expertise. The Inquiry gathered each month, not in a shared physical space as we would have hoped – not in a meeting house, or a hall, or a library, or a field – but on Zoom, where the whole world gathers these days, and in those Zoom calls the questions that must be asked of arbitrary detention were raised.

Like the stories themselves, the films and the subsequent deliberations are difficult, because the effect of detention is to break people down. In response to the question, for instance, How are people detained? – the purpose of which was to detail the process and practices that constitute detention – a number of people with lived experience of detention reported the difficulty of living in cells in which the lights are left on 24 hours a day. Imagine the effect of continuous exposure to light, the way, on a daily basis, it must mess with a person's head. In the films and the discussions, people who had experienced detention also spoke of the traumatic effect of being repeatedly taken to, and returned from, the waiting area for deportation. Think about that, being toyed with in this way. And think about the fact that in 2020 – even against the draconian standards of the UK's Hostile Environment – over 60 per cent of people who were detained were subsequently released. In her film addressing the same question (How are people detained?) made for the Walking Inquiry, Dr Lucy Williams reported that, unlike in any other area of the UK's carceral system, people are detained – and moved around the detention centre estate – in the middle of the night. Perhaps this is because it's cheaper, because as a privatised enterprise the detention estate is driven by profit. This is why people who are not allowed to work when in the community are permitted to work while in detention for £1 per hour. But then remember the reason that people are not moved (let alone detained) at night in *other* parts of the carceral system is that to move people in that way is deemed too traumatic.

And consider that what people who have experienced detention say repeatedly, which surely should not be a surprise – and which surely any inquiry into detention should put front and centre – is that the sheer arbitrariness of the process is almost too much to bear. It is a process framed by the fact that every time – typically every week – a person 'signs' at a Home Office Reporting Centre, on each and every one of those occasions they might be detained (again). It is a process framed by the fact, also, that once a person finds themselves detained, then from day to day, or month to month, they will not know when they might be released. And by the fact that through this whole period of not knowing when they might be released, a person will frequently be threatened (albeit disingenuously) with deportation. Almost too much to bear. Or, for some people, simply and brutally too much. In December 2020, *The Guardian* reported that 29 people seeking asylum died that year in Home Office accommodation.[5]

The Walking Inquiry will publish its findings later this year. What provisional submissions to that Inquiry show is that in the detention estate 'inhuman or degrading treatment' cannot be limited to a five-month period in a single centre. Detention itself is an abuse. It is what takes shape when human rights are disregarded. And it takes the form that it does because once a political system disregards human rights, it will dehumanise those to whom human rights are not permitted to apply.

The International Environment

In 2020, because of the social distancing necessitated by the pandemic, it wasn't possible for Refugee Tales to walk en masse. At that point in the emergence of the virus, people could gather in small groups, but like all other large-scale public events, Refugee Tales 2020 had to be re-thought. The view was that the walk shouldn't stop, that as people who had been arbitrarily detained were just as suddenly rendered destitute when COVID-19 outbreaks in detention centres required their release, some version of the project should be sustained. The result was that the walk dispersed. Instead of gathering in one location and collectively following a shared route, people walked where they could, drawn together across a three-day weekend by a series of online events: talks calling for A Future Without Detention, given by a combination of people with lived experience and other contributors associated with the project, such as Shami Chakrabarti, Angie Hobbs, Kamila Shamsie, Jonathan Wittenberg; films, including 'Roadmaking' and 'Azure', by Ali Smith and Sarah Wood; and tales told in the first person and in collaboration with writers, Christy Lefteri, Robert Macfarlane, Dina Nayeri, Simon Smith. To mark where people were walking, the project plotted their locations on an online map, and what the map showed was that by the end of the event people had walked in support of a call for A Future Without Detention in over 20 countries worldwide.

What the extent of that participation indicates is that, while the detention regime in the UK is singularly abusive, it is nonetheless part of a deeply troubling international pattern. Witness the fact that the growth in the UK detention population over the past two decades is mirrored elsewhere in the Anglophone world. In the US, as the Global Detention Project reports, 'The number of people placed in detention annually increased from some 85,000 people in 1995 to a record 477,523 during the fiscal year 2012'. As in the UK, the US figure has fallen somewhat from that historic high, standing at 323,591 in 2017. One explanation for that decrease, as The Global Detention Project reports US officials as claiming, is the reduction in 'unauthorized arrivals', a measure in itself of an increasingly aggressive border regime. A similar graph can be drawn in the case of Australia, which, as has been well reported, externalises the process by the practice of off-shoring detention and where (unlike in the US and the UK) detention is mandatory for all non-citizens without a valid visa. As part of the 2020 walk, Refugee Tales was honoured to screen talks by the novelist Behrouz Boochani and his translator Omid Tofighian, in which they spoke about the brutal conditions of detention on Manus Island, to which Boochani's novel *No Friend But the Mountains* is a brilliant and devastating response.

Such rates of increased detention should be deeply alarming. Really to grasp their significance, however, we have to hear them not piecemeal, as the result of the practices of individual regimes and governments, but as elements in a profoundly disturbing transnational trend. Consider how frequently in the present moment news reporting turns to the question of detention, always in outrage that these practices are occurring elsewhere. Consider, for instance, as various news outlets and agencies are reporting at the moment of writing: that India has detained scores of Rohingya refugees ahead of anticipated deportation to Myanmar; that the Biden administration has reopened a Trump-era detention site for migrant children; that inspectors have condemned COVID-19 protection, fire safety and living conditions at the Napier and Penally barracks in the UK. And then start scaling up. Start to think about the numbers of people for whom some form of detention, though not their immediate reality, exists as a constant structural threat. This number will include people whose documents are not in order and might therefore either be working illegally, or might be waiting, endlessly, forbidden to work. It will include, for instance, undocumented migrants in the US who, though integral to their local economy, know that they can be detained at any moment, subject for instance (as 'The Pruner's Tale' documented in *Refugee Tales Volume III*) to a driver's license check by Immigration and Customs Enforcement (ICE). It is difficult to gain a perspective on the scale of this kind of existence, in which precarity arising from a fraught relation to national setting is framed and underwritten by the fact or prospect of some form of protracted incarceration – whether in detention centres, removal facilities, or various forms of camp – but recent figures start to help. In the year ending 2019, the United Nation's High Commissioner for Refugees (UNHCR) reported that 79.5 million people were displaced, which is to say one person in every 100 people. Not all of those displaced are forced to seek an existence in another country, and not all of those who are displaced to another country meet with structural prohibition. In Uganda, for example, currently host to the largest refugee operation in Africa, refugees have 'the right to work and establish businesses and access to services such as health care and education'.[6] Even so, the UNHCR statistics for the year ending 2019 indicate the scale of the issue at hand. To speak about detention in the present moment is to speak about an intensifying global condition.

Writing in 2005 in *State of Exception*, his short history of arbitrary detention, the philosopher Giorgio Agamben issued the following warning:

> the state of exception tends increasingly to appear as the dominant paradigm of government in contemporary politics. This transformation of a provisional and exceptional measure into a technique of government threatens radically to alter – in fact, has already palpably

altered – the structure and meaning of the traditional distinction between constitutional forms. Indeed, from this perspective, the state of exception appears as a threshold of indeterminacy between democracy and absolutism.

A 'state of exception' is a setting in which people are subject to the force of the law, but where they cannot apply to the law's protections. Arbitrary detention is the paradigm case. To detain in this way, as Agamben warned, was to stand at the threshold of indeterminacy between those two kinds of regime, to alter the traditional distinction between the constitutional forms.

Since Agamben's book was published, and as he warned that it would, the paradigm of the state of exception has been extended. As the escalating use of detention as a means of controlling human movement shows, regimes of all kinds now deem it acceptable to detain non-citizens *en masse*, on the grounds, simply, that they come from somewhere else.

It is in order to challenge detention both nationally and internationally that *Refugee Tales IV* contains a series of international tales. By bringing together tales from Canada, Greece, Italy and Switzerland, the volume points to the need for shared and combined calls. The use of detention spreads. One regime gives permission to another. Its serial adoption could hardly be more corrosive to the principle of human rights. It can be difficult to imagine in our bordered world, but what the situation calls for is solidarity, a shared insistence, wherever it occurs, that people must not be detained.

Calling for a Future without Detention

The publication date of *Refugee Tales IV* marks a significant international anniversary. 70 years ago to the day, on 28 July 1951, representatives of 26 countries signed the *Convention Relating to the Status of Refugees*. Since the adoption of the Convention in 1954, and of the subsequent 1967 Protocol, 142 countries have become signatories to the Convention, the

149

intention of which was to affirm and extend the principles of the *Universal Declaration of Human Rights*. As the preamble to the Convention states, where the Universal Declaration had affirmed the principle that 'human beings shall enjoy fundamental rights and freedoms without discrimination', the 1951 Convention set out to 'assure refugees the widest possible exercise of these fundamental rights and freedoms'.

We can read the significance of the 70th Anniversary of the 1951 Convention in substantively different ways. The document's aim, as the UN High Commissioner for Refugees Sadako Ogata stated in 1991, was to establish 'the most comprehensive legally binding international instrument, defining standards for the treatment of refugees'. Fundamental to those standards was the principle of non-refoulement, which is to say the prohibition of expulsion or return. As Article 23 of the Convention states:

Prohibition of expulsion or return ('refoulement')
1. No Contracting State shall expel or return ('refouler') a refugee in any manner whatsoever to the frontiers of territories where his life or freedom would be threatened on account of his race, religion, nationality, membership of a particular social group or political opinion.

Mass, arbitrary, protracted detention, underwritten by the constant threat of removal, and continuous with a post-detention existence that, as the stories here show, is rendered barely tenable, is a breach of the intention of Article 23. If persons held in these circumstances are not necessarily returned – though the drive to remove, return and re-displace is intense – they remain, in every legal, political and institutional sense, expelled. They are held outside all normal modes of interaction. They are punished for their national status or because of their race. It is, moreover, a drive to expel that seems set to intensify. As *Refugee Tales IV* goes to press, the UK government has just published its Sovereign Borders Bill, a key provision of which is that any person who might secure asylum in the UK (as opposed to persons who might be selected for asylum out of country) will remain permanently subject to deportation. What this would mean, if it is carried out, is that from the UK's point of view, a person can't flee. What it would mean, if they do flee, is that they will be permanently subject to the prospect of being expelled. The mass detention of people who have been displaced and the now unending threat of deportation constitutes a contravention of the 1951 Convention. To observe the document's 70th Anniversary is undeniably therefore to mark a falling off, a dereliction of the UK's commitment to human rights.

Except that, as Shami Chakrabarti's Prologue to this book reminds us so powerfully, what that document also demonstrates is that such acts of political imagination as the Convention are possible; that in the face of the greatest crisis of forced displacement the world had ever witnessed, and in the wake of a global conflict driven by the politics of nation, it was possible, because necessary, to reassert the values of human recognition, to establish the principle that no-one shall be expelled. The 1951 Convention is an act of what Ali Smith has memorably called 'the better imagined', and its 70th anniversary is a historic reminder that we can imagine better again.

To do that imagining it is necessary, always, to share the stories. If you need evidence that sharing the stories of people who have experienced detention is necessary to ending detention, consider the lengths political regimes of all kinds go to in order to shut those stories down. Detention itself is a shutting out of stories, a way of isolating those whose stories the state doesn't want heard. The culture of constant fear which constitutes the Hostile Environment is a way of stopping those stories from coming out. Because to hear the stories of people with lived experience of detention is to know that detention has to end. Where human rights are denied there is always a silencing of stories because, inconvenient as it is for states to acknowledge, rights have force.

Which is not to suggest, as Refugee Tales would never suggest, that it is sufficient simply to share stories. The project's aim, rather, is constantly to extend the space in which such stories can properly be heard. The stories shared in this volume – whether written in the first person or, because of the ongoing threat to individuals' safety, co-produced with writers – communicate the realities of detention and the ongoing impact of those realities on individual lives. What the stories help generate and underpin is a widening space in which the stories of people who have experienced detention can be heard and shared. These stories combine with the films Ridy Wasolua has made as part of the Walking Inquiry, which share personal accounts of the lived experience of detention and post-detention life. These stories in turn underpin the work of the Refugee Tales self-advocacy parliamentary lobbying group. And all of these stories are part of the increasingly international network against detention, of which the Refugee Tales project is part. Where rights are denied, stories are silenced. Which does not mean that the sharing of stories entails the securing of rights. What it does mean is that the act of sharing stories cannot stop.

And nor can the walking because, as the project walks, so in walking, it looks to reclaim the ground. The ground is solidarity to which the sharing of stories is crucial. The walk continues. Detention must end.

David Herd,
May, 2021

Notes

1. Daniel Wilsher, *Immigration Detention: Law, History, Politics* (Cambridge: Cambridge University Press, 2012), p.88.

2. See https://www.gov.uk/government/statistics/immigration-statistics-april-to-june-2015/detention. Accessed on 12 April, 2021.

3. See https://www.gov.uk/government/statistics/immigration-statistics-year-ending-march-2020/how-many-people-are-detained-or-returned. Accessed on 12 April, 2021.

4. Panorama were able to broadcast this report with the help of guard-turned-whistleblower, Callum Tulley.

5. Diane Taylor, *The Guardian*, 15 December, 2020. See https://www.theguardian.com/uk-news/2020/dec/15/revealed-shocking-death-toll-of-asylum-seekers-in-home-office-accommodation. Accessed on 12 April, 2021.

6. See https://reporting.unhcr.org/uganda. Accessed 12 April, 2021.

About the Contributors

Bidisha is a broadcaster, journalist and film-maker. She specialises in human rights, social justice and the arts and offers political analysis, arts critique and cultural diplomacy tying these interests together. She writes for the main UK broadsheets and broadcasts for BBC TV and radio, ITN, CNN, ViacomCBS and Sky News. Her fifth book, *Asylum and Exile: Hidden Voices of London*, is based on her outreach work in UK prisons, refugee charities and detention centres. Her first short film, *An Impossible Poison*, received its London premiere in March 2018 and has been selected for numerous international film festivals. Her latest publication is called *The Future of Serious Art* and her latest film series is called *Aurora*.

Shami Chakrabarti is a human rights lawyer, campaigner, life peer and privy counsellor. She was the director of Liberty (the National Council for Civil Liberties) from 2003 to 2016 and the Shadow Attorney General from 2016 until 2020. She is a Master of the Bench of the Middle Temple and carried the Olympic Flag at the London Games in 2012. She was formerly Chancellor of Oxford Brookes University and the University of Essex. She has written, spoken and broadcast widely and is the author of two books: *On Liberty* (2014) and *OfWomen* (2017). Both are published by Penguin.

Kyon Ferril was born in Jamaica and has lived in Canada since he was four years old. Currently detained, Kyon is intent on rebuilding his life and community through poetry.

David Herd's collections of poetry include *All Just* (2012), *Outwith* (2012), *Through* (2016), and *Songs from the Language of a Declaration* (2019). His essays and poems have been widely published and his recent writings on the politics of human movement have appeared in *From the European South*, *Los Angeles Review of Books*, *Paideuma*, and the *TLS*. He is Professor of Modern Literature at the University of Kent and a founder and co-organiser of *Refugee Tales*.

HH was granted a two-year residence permit in Italy over five years after he first sought asylum. He lived in Senegal, Lebanon, Egypt, Thailand and speaks five languages fluently. He is currently learning new dialects and new words.

JB was granted asylum for five years in the UK. He lived in Uganda where he hopes to return one day when the dust settles. He is currently a fully qualified plumber and is training to be a gas engineer, a course he says has helped him transform into a new person, more than just an asylum seeker, and has also made him busy enough to avoid thoughts of what he went through.

Brought up in London, **Christy Lefteri** is the child of Cypriot refugees. She holds a PhD in creative writing from Brunel University, where she is now a lecturer. Her novel, the international bestseller *The Beekeeper of Aleppo*, won the Aspen Words Literary Prize and was the runner-up for the Dayton Literary Peace Prize. She is also the author of *A Watermelon, a Fish and a Bible*, which was longlisted for the IMPAC Dublin Literary Award. Her latest novel, *Songbirds*, is published July 2021.

Robert Macfarlane is the author of books about people, place and nature including *Underland, The Old Ways, The Wild Places* and, with the artist Jackie Morris, *The Lost Words* and *The Lost Spells*. He is a Fellow of Emmanuel College, Cambridge.

Khodadad Mohammadi was born and raised in Daykundi province in Afghanistan. He left Afghanistan in January 2016 and has been in Germany since November 2020.

Dina Nayeri is the author of *The Ungrateful Refugee*, winner of the Geschwister Scholl Preis and finalist for the *Los Angeles Times* Book Prize, the Kirkus Prize, and *Elle* Grand Prix des Lectrices. Her essay of the same name was one of *The Guardian's* most widely read long reads in 2017. A fellow at the Columbia Institute for Ideas and Imagination in Paris, and winner of the 2018 UNESCO City of Literature Paul Engle Prize, Dina has won a National Endowment for the Arts grant, the O. Henry Prize, and Best American Short Stories, among other honours. Her work has been published in 20+ countries and in the *New York Times*, *The Guardian*, *The Washington Post*, *The New Yorker*, *Granta*, and many other publications. She is a graduate of Princeton, Harvard, and the Iowa Writers Workshop.

Anna Pincus is a founder and coordinator of Refugee Tales and has worked with people in immigration detention for over fifteen years. She is currently Director of Gatwick Detainees Welfare Group.

Amy Sackville teaches Creative Writing at the University of Kent, and writes fiction and other prose. She is the author of three novels, most recently *Painter to the King* (Granta, 2018).

Philippe Sands QC is Professor of Law at University College London and a practising barrister at Matrix Chambers. He appears as counsel before international courts and tribunals, and sits as an international arbitrator. He is author of *Lawless World* (2005) and *Torture Team* (2008) and numerous academic books on international law, and has contributed to the *New York Review of Books*, *Vanity Fair*, the *Financial Times*, *The Guardian* and the *New York Times*. His latest books are *East West Street: On* *the Origins of Crimes Against Humanity and Genocide* (2016) (awarded the 2016 Baillie Gifford Prize, the 2017 British Book Awards Non-Fiction Book of the Year, and the 2018 Prix Montaigne) and *The Ratline: Love, Lies and Justice on the Trail of a Nazi Fugitive* (2020), also available as a BBC podcast. Philippe is President of English PEN and a member of the Board of the Hay Festival of Arts and Literature.

Rachel Seiffert has published four novels, *A Boy in Winter*, *The Dark Room*, *Afterwards*, and *The Walk Home*, and one collection of short stories, *Field Study*. In 2003, she was named one of Granta's Best of Young British Novelists, and in 2011, she received the EM Forster Award from the American Academy of Arts and Letters. Her novels have been shortlisted for the Booker Prize, the Dublin/IMPAC Award, and longlisted three times for the Women's Prize for Fiction, most recently in 2018. She currently teaches at Birkbeck, University of London, and runs workshops for young writers with First Story.

Natalia Sierra was born on a island in the Caribbean Sea and grew up in Bogota. In 2016, she fled Colombia with her family to seek asylum in Switzerland and waited four years to be recognised as a refugee.

Simon Smith is a poet who lives in London. His most recent books appeared in 2018: *The Books of Catullus* (Carcanet), *DAY IN DAY OUT* (Parlor Press) and *Some Municipal Love Poems* (Muscaliet Press). In January 2020 he appeared on the Radio 4 programme 'In Our Time' to speak about Catullus.

Maurizio Veglio is a clinical faculty member at the International University College (IUC) of Turin and a lawyer – admitted to the Turin bar – specialising in immigration law. Since 2011 he has been a lecturer at the Human Rights and Migration Law Clinic (HRMLC). He is author of articles and contributions on the topic of asylum, administrative detention, legal storytelling and cultural translation. In 2014 he co-authored the textbook *Lo straniero e il giudice civile* (Utet). Among his recent works are: *Uomini tradotti. Prove di dialogo con richiedenti asilo* (Diritto, immigraziomne e cittadinanza), *L'attualità del male. La Libia dei Lager è verità processuale* (Seb27, 2018) and *La malapena. Sulla crisi della giustizia al tempo dei centri di trattenimento degli stranieri* (Seb27, 2020).

Acknowledgements

The editors would like to thank everyone with lived experience of detention who has shared their tale in this book. Thank you to the writers. Thank you to everybody who was walked with Refugee Tales and to Izzy Sutherland, Mary Sutton, Josie Wade, Frances Bell, Mary Barrett, John Barrett, Christina Fitzsimons and all involved in the planning of the project. Thank you to Ricardo Vilela, Chris Orange and everyone who made the 2020 Refugee Tales Online possible. Thank you to the British Academy, whose funding for the Hostile Environments project has enabled us to include international tales. Thank you to our international collaborators: Claudia Gualtieri, Maurizio Veglio, Lidia De Michelis, Steve Collis, Ayendri Riddell, Erin Goheen Glanville, Bethany Rielly, Sapphire Allard, Erol Balkan and Maddy Adams. Thank you to The Orange Tree Trust and Comic Relief whose funding has made the Walking Inquiry possible. Thank you to Ridy Wasolua, Antonia Bunin and everyone who was worked to make the Walking Inquiry happen. Thanks to the University of Kent. Thank you to everyone at Comma Press for your support for Refugee Tales. Thank you to Gatwick Detainees Welfare Group and all the people GDWG has worked with in detention whose experiences inspired Refugee Tales. Thanks to our patron Abdulrazak Gurnah and thank you to our patron Ali Smith.

Refugee Tales: Volume I

978-1-91097-423-0 • £9.99

Featuring: Patience Agbabi, Jade Amoli-Jackson, Chris Cleave, Stephen Collis, Inua Ellams, Abdulrazak Gurnah, David Herd, Marina Lewycka, Avaes Mohammad, Hubert Moore, Ali Smith, Dragan Todorovic, Carol Watts & Michael Zand

Refugee Tales: Volume II

978-1-91097-430-8 • £9.99

Featuring Caroline Bergvall, Josh Cohen, Ian Duhig, Rachel Holmes, Jackie Kay, Olivia Laing, Helen Macdonald, Neel Mukherjee, Alex Preston, Kamila Shamsie & Marina Warner

Refugee Tales: Volume III

978-1-91269-711-3 • £9.99

Featuring Monica Ali, Lisa Appignanesi, David Constantine, Bernardine Evaristo, Patrick Gale, Abdulrazak Gurnah, David Herd, Emma Parsons, Ian Sansom, Jonathan Skinner, Gillian Slovo, Lytton Smith, Roma Tearne & Jonathan Wittenberg

God 99

Hassan Blasim

Chess-playing people-traffickers, suicidal photographers, absurdist sound sculptors, cat-loving rebel sympathisers, murderous storytellers... The characters in Hassan Blasim's debut novel are not the inventions of a wild imagination, but real-life refugees and people whose lives have been devastated by war. Interviewed by Hassan Owl, an aspiring Iraq-born writer, they become the subjects of an online art project, a blog that blurs the boundaries between fiction and autobiography, reportage and the novel.

Framed by an email correspondence with the mysterious Alia, a translator of the Romanian philosopher Emil Cioran, the project leads us through the bars, brothels and bathhouses of Hassan's past and present in a journey of trauma, violence, identity and desire. Taking its conceit from the Islamic tradition that says God has 99 names, the novel trains a kaleidoscopic lens on the multiplicity of experiences behind Europe's so-called 'migrant crisis', and asks how those who have been displaced might find themselves again.

Translated from the Arabic by Jonathan Wright.

'*Sprawling and breathtaking, stuffed with cultural and literary references, this is a dazzling work of imagination and ur-reality.*'
– The Irish Times

'*A storehouse of revulsion and wonder.*'
– The Morning Star

ISBN: 978-1-90558-377-5
£9.99

The Book of Ramallah

Edited by Maya Abu Al-Hayat

Unlike most other Palestinian cities, Ramallah is a relatively new town, a de facto capital of the West Bank allowed to thrive after the Oslo Peace Accords, but just as quickly hemmed in and suffocated by the Occupation as the Accords have failed. Perched along the top of a mountainous ridge, it plays host to many contradictions: traditional Palestinian architecture jostling against aspirational developments and cultural initiatives, a thriving nightlife in one district, with much more conservative, religious attitudes in the next. Most striking however – as these stories show – is the quiet dignity, resilience and humour of its people; citizens who take their lives into their hands every time they travel from one place to the next, who continue to live through countless sieges, and yet still find the time, and resourcefulness, to create.

Featuring: Liana Badr, Ahlam Bsharat, Ameer Hamad, Maya Abu Al-Hayat, Khaled Hourani, Ahmad Jaber, Ziad Khadash, Ibrahim Nasrallah, Anas Abu Rahma, Mahmoud Shukair

'*The Ramallah of this collection feels something like a big bus terminal, with people coming and going, confused about whose seat is whose, and where often travel is shut down entirely. And yet there are also moments of wicked humour, tender love, and elevating grace.*'
– Middle East Eye

ISBN: 978-1-91269-742-7
£9.99